988

D0398946

DOUBLE
DOG
D·A·R·E

DOUBLE DOG D·A·R·E

BY JAMIE GILSON
Illustrated by Elise Primavera

LOTHROP, LEE & SHEPARD BOOKS
NEW YORK

First Edition   1 2 3 4 5 6 7 8 9 10

Library of Congress Cataloging in Publication Data
Gilson, Jamie. Double dog dare.
Summary: The fifth grade year gets off to a busy start as one student
returns from winning a national Miss Pre-Teen Personality contest, a new
girl with some interesting knowledge arrives, jealousy gets a grip on one
particular student, and an "experiment" to see who's smart is conducted.
[1. Schools—Fictional] I. Primavera, Elise, ill. II. Title.
PZ7.G4385Dp 1988   [Fic]   87-37855
ISBN 0-688-07969-5

To Tom, really TAG

Contents

DOUBLE
DOG
D·A·R·E

1

Skipping Miss Wonderful

"I dare you," Nick said, turning around and grinning. His finger was touching the doorbell, ready to push. "What you've got to do is fling the spider at Molly as soon as she opens the door. Then she'll scream, and we'll run. OK?"

I crossed my eyes at him. All the way to Molly's house Nick and I had been playing catch with my black rubber spider. It was as big as my hand and twice as sticky. "You know Molly won't scream at this," I told him. "It's fake. She'd make a *real* one turn and run. Miss Muffet she's not."

"OK, how about if I forget pushing the bell," Nick said, "and we just go home. I still can't believe we're going to this party."

"I told her we would," I explained again. "Besides, it's not really a party. Molly just said she'd asked everybody over. And it's the last summer thing before school starts Tuesday. Don't back out on me now."

"*Everybody* will be here?" he asked.

"That's what Molly said." I could see a light in the living room and people moving around.

"OK, if you want to, we'll go in, but throw the spider anyway." He leaned on the bell, which went ding-dong, and we swung back to hide on either side of the door. We were laughing like crazy because, even if Molly didn't scream, she wasn't going to love getting eight sticky legs on her chin.

We waited, trying to swallow our laughs, and soon we heard the knob click and the screen door swing open. For a long breath nobody said anything, then we wheeled around fast to the door yelling "WOOOOAHH!" and I let the spider fly. I let the spider fly just before I saw who was standing there. It was Molly Bosco's grandmother.

Nick made a funny high noise in the back of his throat that sounded like "Eeep." I swallowed hard.

You don't throw spiders at grandmothers. Normally. Although my mother would say it's a hard and fast rule.

Of course Mrs. Bosco isn't just any old grandmother. For openers, she's not a little old gray-haired lady like the one the wolf ate in Little Red Riding Hood. She has very black hair that makes you think of bats' wings and she's so big it would take two wolves, maybe three, to eat her up.

She's not a screamer, either. She bellowed. "Oh, you two are scamps," she howled. "I always tell Molly that Hobie Hanson and Nick Rossi are such scamps!" The spider was caught in her hair like a Halloween hat. It wiggled when she laughed. "I did think, though, that since you're starting fifth grade next week, you'd have learned to be a little more grown up." She plucked the spider off her head, shook it at my face, and then stuck it to the back of my neck. A field of goose bumps popped up for it to sit on.

"Hello, Mrs. Bosco," I said. "I'm sorry about the spider." I could feel its feet slowly moving, but I wasn't about to reach for it. "We didn't know it would be you."

"Hobie was planning to scare, you know . . ." Nick told her.

"Molly?" she asked. "Oh, well," she went on, laughing even louder, "that's much more grown up, isn't it? Molly!" she called. "You have guests." She smiled at the creature crawling down my neck. "Three of them." And she headed up the steps, patting at her hair.

"We're in here," Molly called. I grabbed the spider and shoved it into my pocket.

In the living room Molly was sitting on a red plaid sofa with a sack of microwave popcorn and a bowl of grapes in front of her. Her arms were folded tight. She did not look happy.

Everybody was *not* there. Michelle and Jenny, two kids from our old fourth-grade class, were the only other ones. They were sitting on the rug looking at TV. I felt dumb.

"Anybody else coming?" Nick asked Molly.

She shrugged her shoulders. "Who's to know?"

"You got here just in time," Jenny told us.

It was almost seven o'clock and Molly had said to get there by seven. Everybody knew that was when Lisa Soloman, *the* Lisa Soloman from our class, was going to be on TV live all the way from Studio City, California. We live in Stockton, Illinois, so it was a pretty big deal.

"You going to tape it?" Michelle asked Molly. "I mean, it's really historic. Don't you think? Even if you don't like Lisa anymore?" Michelle scooted closer to the television set where a *Beverly Hillbillies* rerun was rerunning.

"You've only got five minutes to load the tape," Jenny warned Molly. "Isn't it crazy, just five more minutes and Lisa will be on TV? All fourth grade she was sitting with us in Mr. Star's room, and now billions and billions of people will be watching her. Coast to coast. Sea to shining sea." Jenny sighed and sat down cross-legged on the floor next to Michelle. They leaned in close enough to make nose prints on the TV screen. The sound track laughed, but they didn't.

"You've *got* a tape, don't you?" Michelle turned around to ask Molly.

"Of course I've got one," Molly said, picking up the remote control. "But why should I tape her? I don't think I'll even watch." She got a major serious look on her face. "Television rots the brain. Medical science has proved it. I saw this show about TV brain rot just a few weeks ago on channel eleven. I bet Hobie and Nick don't want their brains to shrivel up and break into little pieces and drop out their noses." She turned to me. "Do you, Hobie? Is Lisa on television worth *that*?" She got up and walked toward the set.

She'd probably made it up, but it was hard to tell for sure. I shrugged my shoulders and poked Nick, who snuffed in a deep breath like he was trying to keep his brain from sliding out. He grabbed the sack of popcorn and we sank down in the sofa to eat.

Molly sighed and pushed a button on the remote control. "I just wouldn't want to be the one to turn us all into vegetables," she said. The picture sucked away into the center of the screen. She smiled. Then, lifting the control over her head like she was the Statue of Liberty and it was the torch, she made an announcement: "For our own good, I have decided that we will skip Little Miss Wonderful on TV tonight. So will millions of other people, if they're smart. Not that all that many actually get Kids Kable."

The two girls narrowed their eyes at Molly and set their jaws.

"Mostly six-year-olds watch it," I agreed. Kids Kable is pretty tame. Lots of talking animals on it who fall off cliffs and run into trees.

"We're here, though," Nick said with his mouth full.

Molly frowned. "I'll think of something better for us to do."

With the TV giving us this blank square, there wasn't anything to do but eat. Nick gave me a look and I nodded. We'd leave as soon as we finished the popcorn.

"Turn that TV back on right now," Michelle yelled. "Or I'm going home. You're no fun, Molly Bosco."

"Think about it," Molly said. "Almost anything would be more fun than watching Lisa try to be cute." She put the TV control behind her back. "We could swing each other around to see who passes out. *That* would be more fun. We could memorize all fifty official state fish in alphabetical order. *That* would be more fun. Nick could tell us all about his fabulous summer at computer camp. *That* would be more fun. We could . . . "

Nick leaned forward, ready to start telling. Jenny stood up. "This isn't fair, you know," she said. "It's the only reason I came over." She curled her hands into fists.

"We could play Truth or Dare," Molly went on.

"With *boys*?" Michelle yelled. "You've got to be kidding."

"Look, Molly," Nick said. "I don't care one way or the other. Hobie dragged me here. But you're the only kid on the block, the only kid we *know*, who's got Kids Kable. So why don't you just turn it on, and if you don't want to watch the pageant you can leave the room."

"You're kidding. It's my house!" Molly said, which was, of course, true.

Nick and I were down to the layer of oily, unpopped kernels at the bottom of the sack, so I reached over to a bowl of gummy worms on the side table and picked a half-orange half-cherry one up by its tail. Then I snuck the spider from my pocket and set it like a lid on the bowl. "So, Molly," I began, "this is probably the only time a kid we know is going to be on TV coast to coast, right?" I caught the worm's head between my teeth, stretched it out

till it was about ready to snap, and then let it loose to wiggle slowly up my chin.

"Hobie Hanson, you're gross," Molly said. She lifted the spider off the bowl of worms, plopped it on top of the TV, and sat down in a fat blue chair. Sticking the remote control under the pillow behind her, she crossed her arms like a locked door.

"Maybe Lisa really will be crowned Miss Pre-Teen Personality. Tonight. For all the world to see," Jenny said, moving toward Molly and the chair. "And we'll miss it because of you. Three minutes. It's on in three minutes."

"Please with sugar on it." Michelle was begging. "Lisa is my friend and I'm going to watch. I don't care how jealous you are." She stuck her chin out and headed toward Molly. It looked like the beginning of a really terrific three-girl fight. I poked Nick. He poked me back. We decided to wait awhile before going.

Molly yawned. "Want to play Monopoly?" she asked.

She *was* jealous. Really jealous. Almost two months before, Lisa had won the local Miss Pre-Teen Personality pageant in Stockton. Molly had won first runner-up. But since Lisa hadn't broken her leg or decided to just blow off the whole contest, being first runner-up was worth about as much as a wad of chewed bubble gum.

Lisa then won the state contest and went on to these absolutely final finals in California. Molly sure didn't want to see Lisa actually win the big prize and get a crown that she could and probably would wear every day to fifth grade.

Molly didn't want to see that, but I knew what she *did* want to see.

I flicked a half-popped kernel into her hair. "Maybe," I said, "Lisa'll get so scared with all those little red-eyed cameras staring at her that she'll fall flat on her face."

A corner of Molly's mouth twitched. "You think so?"

Jenny saw the twitch. She backed up and fingered the knobs on the TV set. "Maybe," she said, watching Molly very closely, "when Lisa does the splits for the talent part, her leotard will get the splits, too, and she'll have to run off the stage and die of embarrassment."

"I doubt it," Molly said, but she smiled.

"*Two* minutes," Michelle wailed. "Two. I'm asking you nicely for the last time. Turn it on or else."

11

She was edging behind Molly and the hidden control.

"You know what?" Nick grinned. "I bet when they come to the part where the MC guy asks all the girls questions, he'll ask Lisa what she wants most out of life, and she'll say she wants to make straight A's and be the smartest kid in her class." He shot a small, hard kernel of corn at Molly. It got her on the neck.

"Cut it out," she said. But she laughed out loud. Molly is the smartest kid in our class. She always has been. She would already be asking for extra-credit stuff while Lisa was fighting her way through the first problem. Molly reached under the seat cushion, pulled out the remote control, aimed it at the set, and pushed the ON button.

"*That,*" she said, "would be worth watching," and the TV began, once again, to glow.

2
·•··

Now, How About
You Folks at Home?

"There she is!" Michelle yelled. "Right in the front row. There." She leaned forward and pointed to a spot on the screen where Lisa wasn't anymore.

The girls on TV were dancing. And it was true, Lisa was in the front row. It wasn't easy to find her, though. They'd changed her hair. Or she had. It was all fluffed out like there'd been an explosion of curls on her head. It was green. Her face was green, too. The black girl next to her was darker green. The stars behind them were blinking green in a grass-green sky. It looked like Lisa had turned up in the Emerald City.

"Would you please fix the color?" Michelle asked Molly sweetly. "All that green is making me sick."

"It's not the color that's making you sick," Molly said, but she pushed a few buttons until the picture stopped looking like it was being shot through lime Jell-O.

About fifty Miss State Pre-Teens were shuffle-hopping up and down a silver staircase, flinging their arms from side to side, singing a song about how plain it was to SEE that there was soon to BE a new Miss Pre-Teen PersonaliTY. The dancers were dressed in identical sweat suits with MPTP patches on them. The sweat suits really were green.

You couldn't tell by watching TV, but they must have been terrific dancers and singers in person because the audience was clapping and yelping and stomping and whistling like crazy.

"When we were little, Hobie and I went to a TV studio once to see a Bozo show," Nick said. "The clown in charge told us exactly when to clap and scream. Remember?"

"Shhhhhhh." Jenny turned around and glared at him.

"I remember," I said, laughing. It was still funny, even if it had been a long time ago. We had been in first grade. "I remember how they made us wave at the camera with both arms so it would look like there were twice as many of us." I waved my arms at Nick as though I were two people, and he waved his arms back, and we started breaking up.

"Shhhhhhh," Jenny said again, louder.

"That's what's going on there, then," Molly decided. "Some clown in Studio City is holding up a sign that says APPLAUSE. APPLAUSE." Then she turned in the blue chair and started talking loud at Nick and me. "So, Nick," she asked, "how was camp? Tell me *all* about it."

Jenny and Michelle growled softly but didn't really complain. They were afraid, I guess, that Molly would cut them off without a show. Instead, they leaned in closer. So did I. Best friend or not, I'd heard all I wanted to hear about Nick's hotshot summer at Mighty Byte Computer Camp.

" . . . be back with our adorable ten finalists right after these announcements," the smiling MC said.

"Now, don't go 'way, you hear!" He went away, and I stopped listening after a while because it was a commercial I'd heard a zillion times before.

" . . . spent almost every day fooling around at the computer," Nick was telling Molly. "We were always fixing it so our klutzy teacher would trip over cords and unplug things and mess up other kids' programs. It was so funny. And there was this incredible kid who . . ."

I'd heard about the incredible kid, too, who was in Nick's tent, who was smarter than Einstein, and was already almost in college even though he was only fourteen. Big deal.

"What this incredibly smart kid Roger and me did—"

"Roger and *I*," Molly said.

"OK, Roger and *I*. Anyway, what we did was we each took a million dollars—"

"You're kidding," I said. I hadn't heard that one. "Where'd you get a million dollars? You didn't even have a summer job."

"Not *actually* a million dollars." He gave me this look, like, *Why can't you learn how to keep your mouth shut?* "Roger and me—he's got an IQ like 210. I mean, we're talking astronomical—so, anyway, we each took this *hypothetical* million dollars—"

"Hypothetical?" I asked.

He stared at me like he couldn't believe I'd stopped him again. "It means fake, pretend," he said slowly. "You know, like Monopoly money, the kind you can't go to the store and buy a lollipop with." He was talking to me as if I was this slobbering baby, not his best friend all his life.

Molly laughed. She was laughing at me. *She* knew what the word meant. That's what her laugh said. I guess she thought it was funny that I didn't.

"Anyway," Nick went on, "we both studied the stock market and invested our—pretend—million dollars in lots of different stocks to see who could make the most money."

"Wouldn't you hate to be the judges!" The guy on the TV was back. "Wouldn't you hate to decide on just ten winners among all of these incredible young ladies?" The camera cut to show a whole stage of girls who looked like they hoped this show would never end. The audience clapped and ahhhhhhhed.

"So what happened?" Molly asked Nick, but I could tell she was listening to the TV more than she was to him. She kept the remote control aimed at the set, ready to zap it off if she wanted to. But I don't think she wanted to. I think she had to know if Lisa would be in the top ten.

"All of these sweet little girls are holding their breaths," the MC said, tearing open a big silver envelope. "Maybe you are, too." He winked at us, knowing we were. "And here are the names of our top ten finalists. . . ." His voice was high as he started to read. "Allison Waid, Miss Pre-Teen Personality Minnesota!" She covered her face with her hands and then bounced up to the microphone and waved. "Kumi Tsuzuki, Miss Pre-Teen Personality New Jersey!" She tilted her head back and nodded as though it was exactly what she'd expected.

"So, Nick, what happened?" Molly asked again, but this time she was staring at the set, not even pretending to be interested in what Nick was saying.

Nick didn't notice. *He* was interested in what he was saying. "Well, not a whole lot happened, really. I mean, some of the stocks went up and some of them went down and some of them stayed pretty much the same." He told her which ones had gone up, which ones had gone down, and which ones had stayed pretty much the same. Then he leaned back. "Who do you suppose won?" he asked.

"And, finally, last but not least . . . Miss Pre-Teen Personality Illinois . . . little Miss Lisa Soloman," the MC shouted. Lisa smiled and skipped forward. She didn't even look fake-surprised. "Aren't they great! There you have it, our top ten sparklers. And how about you folks at home? Have you decided who your favorite is?"

"Can't we turn this off?" Molly asked.

"Molly's jealous!" Jenny said.

"Molly's jealous of Lisa," Michelle sang in a sing-song.

"Or she wouldn't be afraid to watch." Jenny kept it going.

Molly turned away.

"But don't make up your minds yet," the MC warned us. "Decide, as the judges will, after you watch their fabulous acts and hear their delightful pre-teen conversation."

"I can hardly wait," Molly said, picking a grape out of a dish and chewing it carefully.

"But first," the MC went on, "let's hear a few well-chosen words about sugarless, cavity-chasing, plaque-pounding new formula Gloride Gum, the official gum of the Miss Pre-Teen Personality Pageant."

"So," Nick shouted, louder than the guy pushing Gloride. "So, who do you think won?"

"Lisa did," Michelle said. "Easy."

"I don't know," Jenny told him. "Maybe that kid from South Carolina who hops instead of walks will get it. What do you think?"

"No, I mean between Roger and I," he said, and both girls looked at him as though they thought he'd eaten way too many gummy worms.

"Roger and *me*," Molly corrected him, but this time he didn't say it her way.

"*You* won," I said, because if that wasn't the answer, he wouldn't have asked the question.

"Right!" He was clearly surprised that I wasn't jumping up and down about it. "I beat out Roger the Brain by big bucks. My dad said it served Roger right. My dad also said it was good experience for me."

"For when you get a million real dollars?" I asked him.

He rolled his eyes.

The girls on the TV had started their fabulous acts. The first was a kid in pink who twirled a baton with flames on both ends of the stick. It was really scary. I mean, what if she dropped it or threw it up and it hit the ceiling and exploded? The MC said she was playing with fire, and Jenny and Michelle and I laughed.

I moved down on the floor and sat with Jenny and Michelle. Molly and Nick kept on talking, hardly looking at the screen even when Lisa flipped herself around the stage in her leopard leotard, which didn't split. It was like her legs had springs built into them and like she was made of the same bendable stuff gummy worms are. She must have spent the whole summer practicing. She was good.

After the ten fabulous acts, the interviews were pretty dull, actually. I mean, the MC guy had read stuff about the girls and asked them questions that you could tell he already knew the answers to. Like he asked this kid if she had pets and she said she had thirty-six of them, including one goat, two horses, five white rabbits, and seven cats that had three fleas each. He wouldn't have asked if she'd only had one plain yellow canary named George.

21

When he got to Lisa, he asked her if she was going to keep up her gymnastics.

"Oh, yes!" she said. "I've already decided to win a gold medal in gymnastics in the next Olympic Games. Either that or in figure skating."

"Oooooooo," the audience cooed right along with the announcer. Molly's mouth dropped open.

"I expect all of your friends at home are really proud of you," the announcer said, sure we all were.

"Can I say hi to them?" Lisa asked, then turned to the camera and said, "Hi." To us. Really to us. It was pretty dumb, but Jenny and Michelle yelled at the screen and waved. I almost did, too. We were her friends back home.

Molly and Nick were talking loudly and looking the other way.

"And there she is, folks," the announcer said, "the gifted and talented Miss Lisa Soloman!" Lisa cartwheeled back to her place in line.

Another Gloride commercial came on and Molly pushed a button to blip out all the sound.

"Gifted and talented, ha!" Molly said to fill the silence. "Very funny they should call her that. Did your parents get a letter this summer, Nick?"

He nodded his head and grinned.

"My folks got lots of letters this summer," Jenny said, getting up to stretch her legs. "Some of them were junk mail, of course, and some of them were bills, but my parents get a lot of mail."

Molly laughed as though that wasn't what she meant at all.

Nick glanced over at me. "I haven't told anybody else about it," he said.

"Lisa is, too, gifted and talented, and I bet she wins." Michelle grabbed the last worm and popped it into her mouth whole.

"Maybe by some weird chance she'll win and maybe she won't, but I bet her parents never get the letter *we're* talking about," Molly told Michelle, and then she giggled like that was the joke of the year. Nick looked kind of nervous, but he laughed, too.

"I don't get it," Jenny said, and they laughed louder. I guess they thought it was funny that she didn't get it. They were making me mad.

When the commercials were over, the MC appeared on the screen, a gold envelope in his hand. Michelle yelled for Molly to turn the sound up. And, with a loud sigh, she did.

" . . . but before I announce the winners," the guy was saying, "I want to assure you that any one of these stellar young ladies would make a terrific Miss Pre-Teen Personality." The camera showed close shots of all ten faces, from the kid at one end who'd done bird calls to Lisa at the other, grinning wide under her new Hollywood hair.

"This is so silly," Molly said.

When the camera had looked at all of them, the MC tore open the envelope. He held up the paper and announced the runners-up first.

"Second runner-up, Miss South Carolina!"

"I *told* you she wouldn't get first," Michelle said.

"And the first runner-up . . ." was Miss California. The crowd, mostly from California, liked that a lot. Applause. Applause.

"And the winner . . ." We were all looking and listening, bending toward the set. Not even Molly and Nick could pretend not to care. They were quiet as the camera swept past the eight waiting girls, their biggest smiles on hold.

" . . . a tiny dynamo, a reflection of the exciting times we live in, a force in our glorious future . . . the new Miss Pre-Teen Personality is . . . Miss Illinois—Miss Lisa Soloman!"

Lisa must have jumped two feet into the air. The

girls next to her grinned fake grins as they watched her step forward. She wasn't crying.

Neither was Molly, but she sure wasn't laughing. "I wonder if they'd let me just skip fifth grade," she said.

Lisa was waving her arms at the screaming crowd. When they quieted down she gave her speech.

"This is really awesome," she began. "I mean, everybody else here was just so much cuter than I am. I mean it. And they were all so, like, talented. Saying Shakespeare and juggling and all. But, anyway . . ." She looked straight into the camera, which moved in for a very close close-up. You could see blue stuff smeared around her eyes. "I promise I will do my best to represent pre-teens everywhere, every day, in every way. And I'm really going to try not to be stuck up. All of us here at the pageant have talked about how bad it is to be stuck up." The girls behind her nodded. "Like, we've had our pictures taken all the time and had interviews with, like, the major media and all. Anyway, it's hard not to be stuck up when people are always telling you how awesome you are, but I'm going to try." And she smiled a small, modest smile. "Thank you," she said.

"She's going to be impossible," Molly groaned. "Absolutely impossible."

Lisa threw a kiss at the screen and the credits rolled past her carefully un-stuck-up face. Miss Pre-Teen Personality first runner-up hugged her.

"The gifted and talented Miss Lisa Soloman," Molly said. "We'll see about that."

3
..●..
You Got Who?

Every first day since first grade I've walked to school with Nick and we've talked about who we wanted to get for a teacher and how awful it'd be if we didn't get in the same class. Sometimes we got the same teacher and sometimes we didn't, but even when we didn't we were still best friends.

This first day, though, Nick and I were walking together, but we weren't talking about school. We were talking about the weather. It was weird.

"So, hot enough for you?" he asked me.

"I guess," I said. "How about you?"

"Same," he said, and we didn't talk again for about a block. We just kicked at loose stones on the sidewalk. "So, how was Toledo?" he asked after a while.

"It was OK," I told him. Toledo is where my grandma lives. We'd just gotten back from there because, what with Labor Day and all, there was this long weekend before school started, so my folks decided to just take off and go. "I only got carsick once," I told him. "Even though practically the whole way there I was reading this book in the backseat about a kid who ate worms—real worms, not the grape kind."

"I read that in second grade. It was gross. What did you do in Toledo? Did you have a nice time?" he asked me. They were the wrong questions, the kind of polite questions a grown-up would ask.

"It was OK," I said again. Ordinarily I would have told him all about it. I mean, Toledo wasn't Disneyland, but it wasn't all that bad. There weren't any kids at my grandma's house, so I sat around and looked through boxes of old stuff. I found pictures of my dad at this high-school dance. He wasn't there with my mother, either, even though she went to the same school. He was with this other person who had eyes that made her look like a raccoon. Anyway, besides that, we ate supper one time on a big paddleboat on the river. A Tom Sawyer kind of boat, my dad said. I didn't tell Nick that, either. "How was Fido?" I asked him finally, so he wouldn't have a chance to say, "My, how you've grown," or something equally dumb.

Before we'd left Saturday morning, I'd taken our house key over to Nick so he could come in and feed Fido, my cat. I'd asked him to do that, but I hadn't asked him much else. I hadn't asked him, for instance, about that mysterious letter he and Molly had been laughing about at the party. They were being disgusting. More disgusting than eating real worms with ketchup, or even without ketchup.

"Fido was OK," he told me now. "Except she always hid under the bed when I called her, like I hadn't known her since she was a kitten."

A couple of guys caught up with us and we all walked through the big front doors of the school together. The place smelled the same as it had when we'd left in the spring—like hall wax. Only now the floors were super shiny. Big computer banners said WELCOME TO CENTRAL SCHOOL. We hung out in the front hall talking to guys we hadn't seen all summer and trying not to run right over to take a look at the lists.

Lists of kids' names were posted on a wall near the principal's office. They told you who your teacher was going to be for the year. By the time you got to fifth, though, you didn't fight to get at the lists because you didn't want people to know you cared one way or the other.

Kids all around were being hyper, yelling at each other about camp and other summer stuff.

"You're not going to believe this," a guy was saying, "but there we were in the middle of the street on our skateboards when this . . ."

"I told my mom," I heard one girl say, "that if Molly Bosco is in the same class I'm in again this year, I'll quit school. Only Molly is but I can't because, like my mom says, it's against the law to drop out when you're ten."

There was probably at least one kid in that front hall saying the exact same thing about me. I thought about how great it would be to just go home and crawl under the bed with Fido.

"Hey, Hanson, who'd you get?" R. X. Shea grabbed my elbow. "I got Solberg. He's supposed to be the meanest teacher in school. My sister's best friend had him two years ago when he taught sixth and she said to be sure *not* to get him because he makes you memorize a lot of dates, and he gives hard tests, and he only smiles at parents."

"I don't know who I got," I told him. Nick and the other guys had gone over to check the lists so I figured I'd hear in a minute or two. Actually, I wasn't in any hurry to find out. Chances are they'd hired Godzilla to teach fifth grade, anyway, and I was in for daily blasts of barbecue breath down my neck.

"See, I *can't* be in Solberg's class because I freeze on tests," R.X. said. "I mean it. My mom made me go to this psychologist person last summer to see if I was as stupid as it looked like from the grades I'd been getting. Anyway, he said that I'm really not all that dumb. He said my problem is that I sort of freeze on tests. So, I figure if I sort of freeze on regular teachers' tests, by the time Solberg gets through with me you could ice skate big time down my spine."

"Mr. Solberg never looked mean to me," I said. "A guy I know pretty good had him, and he lived."

R.X. sighed. Then he made a face at a kid behind me. "Well, *you* look mad," he said. "You must have got Solberg, too." I turned around and there was Molly, her face pinched tight.

"I did not get him," she said. "I wanted to be in Mr. Solberg's class. I planned to be in his class. I'm *going* to be in his class. Mr. Solberg has a reputation as a challenging teacher. I've already written his name in my assignment notebook." She flapped a small red pad in our faces. "My grandmother will get me transferred." She glared at me like the whole thing was my fault. "I suppose *you* don't even care."

Actually, she was right. I didn't care. It didn't matter to me one way or the other who Molly got as a teacher. I shrugged my shoulders. "Why should I?"

"Because you got her, too."

"Me?"

"You."

"Got who?"

"*You* know who. I didn't think they'd really do it. My grandmother said this morning at breakfast that fifth grade is the most important year in elementary school. And I don't see how it can be if your teacher

32

is a disaster. I mean, a major disaster. I thought this was supposed to be a good school. They're always giving out pencils stamped with CENTRAL SCHOOL IS NUMBER ONE! Ha, number one!" She was really huffing along. "You know what they want to do to me? Guess!"

"I give up," I said. "Or maybe they want you to take fourth grade over to catch up with the rest of us."

She didn't laugh. "Remember that awful substitute who's supposed to be a real live teacher this year? Miss I'm Gonna Switch," she said. "Well, my name is on her list. And so is yours."

"Miss Ivanovitch? You got Miss *Ivanovitch*?" R.X. said. "You lucky ducks."

"You're kidding!" I couldn't believe it. It was too good to be true. Miss Ivanovitch was this wild sub we'd had in 4B who threw snowballs and paper airplanes and who'd gone with us once on outdoor education. She'd never taught full time before in her life. She'd told us so. And I was going to be in her class.

Bllinnnggg! The warning bell rang loud and long.
"What's the room number?" I asked Molly.

33

"It's two thirteen. Thirteen! That figures. I can't believe this is happening to me."

Neither could I. I dashed up the stairs and rushed down the hall as fast as I could through crowds of kids, most of them wearing new shoes. Fifth grade was going to be a blast.

4

· · ● · ·

Welcome
to Fifth Grade

A picture of a football helmet was taped to the door of room 213. The number on the helmet was 5B. Under it hung a list of names, the kids in 5B. And sure enough, my name was on the list. So was Molly's. So was Lisa's. So was Nick's, though he wasn't there yet.

Across the hall R.X. was heading into Mr. Solberg's room, 5A. "If I don't come up for air by October," he told me, "send in a search party."

"Hey, Hobie, save me a seat," Eugene called from down the hall. His mother was with him. Fifth grade, and his mother still brought him for the first day of school.

I waved and went inside.

Miss Ivanovitch was standing at the front of the room, her name written on the chalkboard behind her in big block letters. On her desk was a vase of bright red roses. Her dress was bright red, too. Her smile was bright, but shaky.

"Hi, Hobie," she said, starting toward me. "I'm glad you're here. You can take a desk anywhere you like."

I rushed to the back of the room, slid into a seat in the last row, and looked around.

Lisa was sitting in front of me. A green Miss Pre-Teen Personality sweatshirt lay spread over her desk like a tablecloth.

"We saw you on TV," I told her. "You were all green at first, but we got you straightened out." She looked at me funny. "Did they tell you to say that stuff about not being stuck up?" I asked her. "So people would clap?"

Shaking her head, she slipped the sweatshirt off

her desk and tied it around her waist so the name didn't show.

"Does everybody, like, hate me?" she whispered.

"Not everybody," I told her. "You know who."

She nodded, untied the sweatshirt, and stuffed it in the desk.

On the bulletin board Miss Ivanovitch had tacked up a lot of pocket folders and a big poster of this zonked-out bear with its head on a football. WAKE UP. READ A BOOK, it said. A girl with short, curly red hair, a girl I'd never seen before, was staring at it.

"And this really smart kid in my cabin and me, we were practically the only ones who . . ." Nick was telling Marshall and another guy as they walked into the room.

Miss Ivanovitch stepped forward. "Take a desk anywhere you like, boys," she said.

Nick stopped where he was, grinned like somebody had just told him a good joke, and then picked up the nearest desk. He was heading out the door with it when Miss Ivanovitch called, "Nick?"

He turned, the desk resting on his stomach, his eyes wide open as though he was surprised she'd spoken. "Yes, Miss Ivanovitch?"

"Nick, perhaps you could tell me where you plan to go with that desk. It's one I like especially well, and I'd hate to lose it on our very first day."

"Well, Miss Ivanovitch, I was thinking that first off I'd like to put it at the free-throw line on the playground," Nick told her.

"The free-throw line?"

"Right. You said."

"*I* said?"

"You said I could take a desk anywhere I liked."

Lisa laughed as if she thought Nick should be crowned Mr. Pre-Teen Stand-Up Comic of the Year. Some other kids laughed, too. Actually, it *was* funny. I clapped.

Miss Ivanovitch smiled. "Somehow, I don't think that would work," she told him. "Dribbling on a desk top requires a certain skill. At least, dribbling a basketball does. You put the desk back where it belongs, and I'll be careful to say exactly what I want— now that I know you'll do exactly what I say."

Nick carried the desk back and bowed to the class like he'd just jumped over eight semi's on his skateboard. When he saw me, he glanced at the empty desk next to mine and then sat with Marshall two rows away. "Maybe we could fit our heads in here," he said loud, and tried to stick his head sideways into the desk hole. The girls laughed again.

That's when Eugene rushed in, trying to pretend his mother wasn't walking into the room behind him. He was wearing a T-shirt that said SURF DOG, but he didn't look much like one. Slipping into the desk next to mine, he studied the tops of his shoes as his mother talked to the teacher. He was still staring at his new, fluorescent laces when she turned to him to wave goodbye.

Just after the final bell rang, Molly strolled in, her face grim. Front-row seats were the only ones left. She took the desk nearest the door.

"Good morning, class," Miss Ivanovitch said brightly. "Welcome to fifth grade. I'm so glad to see you all. I hope you had absolutely wonderful summers. I know Lisa did. I read all about her triumph in the paper today."

Molly cleared her throat and fanned herself with her red notebook.

Lisa smiled carefully. Then she took the Miss Pre-Teen Personality sweatshirt out of the desk and draped it around her shoulders like she'd just noticed an Arctic blast.

"If I've counted right," Miss Ivanovitch said, "all

twenty-five of you are here. Most of you know one another, I think," she went on. And she was right. The kids were a kind of mix from last year's 4A and 4B. "Amber Murnyak has just moved here, though, from Tucson, Arizona. Amber, would you stand up and lead us all in the Pledge of Allegiance."

Amber was the new kid who'd been staring at the poster. She knew the words to the pledge, all right, but her voice shook as she said them.

After we'd finished ". . . with liberty and justice for all," Miss Ivanovitch sat on her desk, leaned forward, and said, "We're going to have a terrific year together. I know it. Have any of you heard what we study in fifth grade?"

"The human body," a kid answered, and everybody laughed.

"Right," she told him. "In science we'll be studying the human body."

"All of it?" Marshall asked, and everybody laughed again.

"Well," she said, "you won't be able to practice medicine when we're through, but I hope you'll know the difference between your aorta and your medulla oblongata."

Molly shrugged like that was old stuff, but I bet

she didn't know the difference or she would have said so. Instead, she raised her hand and asked, "Do we get to dissect frogs?"

"Gross," Eugene whispered.

"It's the human body we're studying," Miss Ivanovitch told Molly, "and frogs aren't human. Unless, of course, you kiss them first. Then the enchanted ones turn to princes."

"Gross," Eugene said again.

"No cutting up frogs," Miss Ivanovitch went on. "That's in junior high. We *will* put a little blood on a slide, though, and take a look at it."

"Sick!" somebody said.

"Do we have to do social studies this year?" Lisa asked.

"We *get* to," Miss Ivanovitch told her. "We're going to fight the French and Indian War on the playground."

"Really?" Lisa asked.

"Well, actually, just pretend. Parents get annoyed if their kids don't come home at night after school."

"Oh," I said, "you mean a *hypothetical* war." I'd show Nick and Molly a thing or two.

The whole room got totally quiet and everybody

turned around and looked at me. A few kids laughed. I was sorry I'd said it.

"Exactly what I mean. I'm impressed," Miss Ivanovitch told me, starting down the aisle and handing out papers. Molly rolled her eyes. I wished I'd kept my mouth shut.

Tucking my head down low, I looked over the long form she'd given us. Name, address, telephone number, birthday, hobbies, favorite subject.

"Can we say recess?" Marshall asked.

Least favorite subject.

"Does social have an *sh* in it?" Lisa asked.

Then Miss Ivanovitch handed out sheets of paper with the schedule for every day. Our whole life sat there in little boxes filled with math, spelling, language arts, science, and stuff. It didn't look like there'd be space to breathe between the lines.

Molly raised her hand. "I don't see the place on here," she said, waving the schedule, "for when I go for my Gifted and Talented class. I expect that's because all of those people are supposed to be in Mr. Solberg's room, and Nick and I are in the wrong place."

Nick cleared his throat like a rock was stuck in it.

Miss Ivanovitch reached over to her desk and picked up a stack of papers. She shuffled through them and pulled out a long yellow sheet. "Oh, you're in the right place, Molly. We'll be spending the whole year together. And, yes," she went on, looking over the yellow paper, "I do see that you are one of the three from this room who are scheduled for TAG."

"Miss . . ." Molly started, and I wondered if she was really going to call her Miss I'm Gonna Switch. Instead, she smiled. Her smile was a little too sweet, though, like she was being kind to a puppy. "Actually, I'm not talking about recess games. I'm talking about serious things. Anyway, in case you didn't know, fifth graders don't play Tag. We stopped playing games like that in second. I'm talking about the new program for . . . for kids who are . . ." She took a deep breath, sat up taller in her chair, and lifted her chin. Then, looking straight at Nick, she said, "For kids who are especially . . . smart."

Nick covered his face with his hands and tried, the way he had before class began, to stick his head in the desk hole. It didn't fit this time, either. But this time nobody laughed.

"What's the matter, Nick? You got, like, a big head?" Lisa asked. Then everybody laughed. Lisa laughed really hard because she knew that's what they'd been thinking about her.

Fifth grade was turning weird from the very first day.

Molly and Nick playing Tag because they're smart? Come on. Tag doesn't take brains. Anyway, Nick wasn't so smart. He got the same kind of grades I did, the kind that when you take them home your folks look at the B in language arts and the C in math and say, "Well, so long as you did your best." At least that's what my folks said. Nick's dad barked at him when he got B's and C's.

"Well?" Molly demanded.

Kids were starting to talk to each other and laugh. Molly sounded like she was the one in charge of the class. Two girls got up and headed toward the pencil sharpener, giggling. Maybe Miss Ivanovitch wasn't going to make it as a real teacher after all.

That's when she picked up a small plastic airplane from her desk and blew into it until the propellers spun and it whistled with a loud *whoEEEEEEEE.* The class turned quiet. "For a really smooth takeoff," she said, "let's just start at the beginning. Special programs don't begin until Monday. Right now it's time to finish your forms."

Molly squirmed in her desk like it was maybe two sizes too small.

Lisa raised her hand. "I lost my pencil," she said. She leaned back in her chair, crossed her arms, and grinned. I guess she thought if Molly was going to try to push Miss Ivanovitch around, so was she.

"I don't have mine, either," I said, because that was true. It was on the kitchen table at home.

"How many of you need a pencil?" Miss Ivanovitch asked. A lot of hands went up, and I thought sure she was going to blast us for not being mature fifth-grade individuals.

"I thought you might. I always forgot my pencil on the first day. I have here, ladies and gentlemen," she went on, picking up a cardboard box, "pencils for the pencil-less." She started passing them to raised hands. "You can keep them. They were cheap. They're rejects from a pencil factory that made mistakes in the printing. That may even explain why they're magic."

Marshall's hand was up to take one. He pulled it back down. "How come magic?" he asked.

"Ah, you'll see as you write," she told him. "These pencils have all the answers."

Lisa showed me hers. It had possibilities. It said TOP KNOT BEAUTY SHOP FOR A BRAND NWE YOU. Wave that over a couple of mice and a pumpkin and who knows? Mine didn't look like a wand, though. It was dark blue smeared with light blue letters: ROPSKI'S BAR AND GRILL. What it needed was an on-off switch, a few blinking lights, and a tiny robot voice that whispered secrets.

Miss Ivanovitch was right. The answers she was looking for flowed straight out of the lead. Amazing. It knew my phone number, address, favorite subject, and name of the kid who could bring me homework if I was out for a week with loose toenails. Nick and I live just a Frisbee toss apart, but the name the pencil wrote was Marshall.

The hardest question was, "Tell me a little about yourself so I can know you better." Sure. "How do you do, my name is Hobie. I'm average. Average height. Average ears. Average stuff in my brain. The only thing about me that's not average is my cat. Her name is Fido."

The pencil didn't know how to draw any better than I did. So I didn't spend much time on the "summer highlight" picture she asked us to draw on a piece of manila paper. I made a couple of squiggles for the Fourth of July fireworks, then stared into the empty desk hole, thinking about Nick and Molly running around on the playground snapping each other with big words and yelling, "Ha, ha. Tag, you're it."

5
····

I Know You Are,
But What Am I?

Lisa pulled the MPTP sweatshirt over her head, fluffed her hair back in place, and stood up. "Miss Ivanovitch, is there time for a really, truly important announcement before the bell rings?"

"There's always time for the truly important," Miss Ivanovitch told her with a small sigh. "First, though, I want all your papers in. It's almost twelve o'clock."

After finishing mine, I'd filled out a whole extra

set—including favorite hobbies—for a kid I'd called Frank N. Stein. Miss Ivanovitch took them without looking. I wondered if she was as glad as I was that the first day of school stops at noon.

"Anyway," Lisa began, turning around so she could look at us all. "I just wanted to say that it isn't my birthday or anything, so you don't have to bring me a present, but my mom is having a, like, party for me Friday night. To celebrate. The reason she's having it is this contest I won, that—in case you hadn't heard—was broadcast live on nationwide TV. From California."

Some kids mumbled about how they'd seen it. Some of them rolled their eyes so she'd know they'd heard she was practically prime time. "Anyway, my mom said she would have this party for me but I couldn't leave anybody out because that would be rude. So I'm inviting everybody in fifth. Like, everybody." She smiled her very-important-person's smile at Molly. Molly didn't smile back.

"Anyway," she went on, "since Friday isn't that far off, I thought I should tell you now. I'll invite the other class tomorrow. So, everybody is supposed to come to the community center at, like, six-thirty Friday, and we'll have pizza and butterscotch brownies in that room they've got for, like, parties, and then we'll all go ice skating. If you've got a pass, bring it with you so this doesn't cost my mom a total fortune. OK? Now I need to know two things. Can everybody come, and is there anybody who doesn't like anchovies?"

A few kids aarged. I couldn't tell if it was because of the party or the anchovies.

Eugene raised his hand. "You mean you're asking boys, too?" In the fourth grade, girls didn't ask boys to parties, that's for sure. *Blinnnggg*. The bell zapped us, and the first day of fifth was gone.

"Boys. Yes, even boys," Lisa called, as everybody pushed out of their seats.

"She means *especially* boys," some girl in front whispered loud.

Miss Ivanovitch waved with both hands. "I'll see you all tomorrow," she said. "Don't forget to bring the supplies on your list."

Nick was heading for the door. "Hey, Rossi!" I yelled, and he turned around. "Wait up, hotshot."

"Look, it's not my fault," he told me when I reached him. "Molly just says all that stuff. Anyway, it's no big deal."

"What *is* it, though, exactly? What's in those letters you and Molly were talking about? All of a sudden you think you're so smart."

Molly covered her mouth, pointing her giggle toward the floor. She was sitting at her desk, waiting for us. "Thinking doesn't have anything to do with it," she said. "We don't think we're smart. We *are* smart. The letter says so. Right here. Right, Nick? Hi, Amber."

That stopped the new kid, who was leaving by herself. "Hi." Her face turned pink. "Hi," she said again, as though maybe the first time hadn't taken. Then she smiled. She had straight teeth with no braces. "This seems like a really friendly school."

"I guess," Nick said.

"I mean," she went on, "people say hello and all. And I thought it was really very nice of that girl— Lisa—to invite everybody in the room to her party. She doesn't even know me."

"Well." Molly lowered her voice like she was telling a secret. "It's *because* you don't know her that you think she's nice. Lisa's just—"

"Are you coming to the party?" I asked the new girl. "Do you like anchovies?"

She laughed. "Maybe she wouldn't have asked me

if she'd known. I scrape anchovies off pizza. Black olives, too. And the only ice I'm good with is cubes. I guess you'll think this is pretty strange, but I've never been ice skating in my life."

"Almost everybody here skates," Molly told her. "But *nobody* likes anchovies except Lisa. They taste like cat food smells. I bet she doesn't even like them. You've got a lot to learn about her. She's always—"

"The inside rink's open all year." I cut Molly off again. My mom would have shouted "Manners!" at me. If this kid wanted to hate Lisa later she could, but it wasn't any of Molly's business. "There's a lot of hockey," I went on, "and, you know, ice nuts who practice about twenty hours a day so they can whirl around with one leg up."

"Lisa tries to whirl," Molly said. "That's why it's a skating party, so Lisa can show off her skirt and her spinning and—"

"When it's cold we skate in the park," I went on. "It's just a flooded field, though, so if you fall through, you only get your ankles wet."

"The weather's never cold enough for frozen fields in Tucson," the new kid told us. "Would you believe I've never even owned a pair of mittens?

Listen, I'd really like to go to Lisa's party so I could get to know people. Do you think it would be OK if I just sat on the side somewhere and watched?"

Molly got up. "I'll take care of you," she said. "Of course I had other plans for Friday night, but I'm going to change my mind and go, just to keep you company."

"Stop it!" a kid called from the hall. "I'm gonna tell. I'm gonna tell." Somebody was crying.

"I did *not*!" a guy yelled. "I didn't do it. It was already broken. It wasn't my fault."

"Liar!" the first voice sobbed. "Liar. Liar. Pants are on fire. Liar! Liar!"

"I know *you* are, but what am I?" the second kid shouted.

Miss Ivanovitch looked up from the stack of papers she was reading on her desk. "Whoa, whoa," she called, and brushed past us out of the room.

I was starting after her to see if maybe there was a bloody nose when Molly said, "Hey, Hobie, don't you want to know what's in the letter?" She smiled. "It's no big secret." Taking a neatly folded paper out of her notebook, she flipped it open. "Want me to read it to you?"

54

What Molly wanted was for the new girl to hear what it said. I grabbed the letter. "I can read." It was on school stationery. Official. It told all about this new program for kids who are gifted and talented. And, big surprise, Molly was one of them. "These are children," it said, "who have demonstrated extraordinary learning capacity as measured by standardized ability and achievement indicators."

I read that part twice, the second time out loud. "OK, I'll bite. What does it mean?" I asked.

"It means they got high scores on tests," Amber said. "That's all."

Molly smiled. "That's plenty." She took the paper from me, folded it back into her notebook, and told the group, "My own personal IQ is 145. My grandmother made them tell her. She says that is very, very high. What's yours?" she asked Nick.

He shook his head. "Nobody told me and I don't care." He turned to the new kid. "How come you knew what that meant?" he asked her.

"I don't know, it's just the way teachers talk sometimes. They had classes like that at my old school. Kids called them EEP. Teachers called them the Extended Enrichment Program."

"Miss Ivanovitch called it TAG," I said.

"Talented And Gifted," Molly explained. "They turned the words around."

"I'd figured that out," I told her. "I like GAT better."

"Look, Hobie, you don't have to feel so bad," Molly said. "Just because our parents got their letters in July doesn't mean your letter won't ever come."

"I *don't* feel bad," I explained. "I don't care. Mine probably got their letter already, only it said I was in this special program the school was setting up just for me. The Dumb and Stupid program."

"You don't need to get mad," Molly told me.

"Excuse me, but I don't have a winter coat yet," the new kid said. "If I do go skating, will I die of frostbite?"

"Let's go." Molly grabbed the new kid's arm and tugged her toward the door. "Hobie's acting weird again. I'll tell you everything you need to know."

And that left Nick and me.

"So, does this mean you get out of regular classes?" I asked him.

"Tuesday and Friday afternoons, the letter said."

"What if that's when the rest of us have social studies?" I asked him.

"I don't know. Let's go home."

"OK, you can tell me. I'm your oldest friend in the world. What's your IQ?"

"I said I don't know, and I don't *care.*"

"Higher than mine, though, or I'd be playing TAG, too, right?"

"Maybe you are, for all I know," he shouted. "Miss Ivanovitch said there were three kids from our class. I'm getting hungry. Are you coming or not?"

"Maybe you should have gone with Molly. You think I'm good enough to walk with you?"

"Stop being so *stupid,*" he yelled, and headed off down the hall.

"I know you are, but what am I?" I yelled back. OK, I knew the answer. If I'm not as smart as Nick, what am I? Stupid. Dumb and stupid. That's what they'll call my special program: Dumb And Stupid backward, SAD.

"Hey, Nick, wait up!" I yelled, but he was already gone.

57

6
Mints Meet

Friday afternoon my mother took a big batch of oatmeal cookies with raisins over to the new girl's house. To welcome the Murnyak family to the neighborhood, she said. She asked me if I wanted to go with her. I told her no, I was busy breathing.

When she came back, my mom told me that Amber was the oldest of four lovely, talented girls: Amber, Beverly, Crystal, and Deirdre. She had told

Mrs. Murnyak that we would be glad to drive Amber to Lisa's party.

"Who's this *we*?" I asked her. "You and Dad?"

"You and me," she said. "And anybody else you want to give a lift. Nick?"

"No," I said. "Not Nick. He thinks he's so smart." I ate a mouthful of crumbs from cookies I'd maimed scooping them off the pan. "It's OK, I guess. If she rides in front with you, I can deal with it."

"Amber seems like such a sweet girl," Mom said, but then Mom thought Molly was sweet.

"Sweet isn't going to help her out much tonight. She's never been on skates before, and she's gonna fall on her face."

"You could, of course, help her," Mom said, but I gave her my sick skunk-that-sprayed-Seattle look. "Well," she went on, "perhaps Molly will hold her up and point her in the right direction. I asked Amber if she'd made any friends, and she said Molly had been very helpful."

Sure, Molly had been helpful. Molly had been treating Amber like her pet poodle. All week at school she'd sat next to Amber and told her where to go next, what to wear when, what to think, and, most of all, who to like and who not to. Then she told everybody that the reason she didn't get herself transferred out to Mr. Solberg's class was so she could take care of poor new Amber. I bet that wasn't it, though. I bet it was because she knew they'd tell her no way she was going to get moved. Our principal, Miss Hutter, isn't big on shifting kids around.

When Mom and I drove up to the curb in front of Amber's house that night, I leaned out the window and yelled, "Hurry up, let's go." Amber was sitting on the front porch steps with her mom and two of her little sisters, twins dressed just alike.

"Now, Hobie, I want you to jump out and walk with her to the car," Mom said.

"You're kidding! She can see where the car is. This isn't a *date*," I told her. "I'm just a kid."

"*My* kid," she said. "And I'm aware it's not a date. I'm just concerned about your manners. I'm your mother. Teaching you manners is my job."

"Hey, wow, will you look at that? She's walking here all by herself. She must be very smart. Doesn't look like she needs my help after all."

"Open the door for her," Mom said.

"Guys don't do that stuff anymore."

"*Open the door.*"

60

I was going to just reach behind me and open it, but Mom gave me The Look. So I went through the whole thing. I got out my door and opened the door to the backseat so Amber could get in.

She was wearing jeans, two sweaters, a long scarf, a red-and-white cap pulled down over her ears, and a pair of what looked like Molly's last winter's red mittens. She got in the backseat.

I was about to get back in the front seat when Mom flipped a switch and locked my door. She smiled, leaned toward me, and said quietly, "Manners." Then she scooted over to the window and started talking to Mrs. Murnyak and the matching kids who had followed Amber down the sidewalk. Mrs. Murnyak wanted to know which plumber would be best for plumbing out their jammed-up drains.

Amber slid over to the far side of the car, looking at her red-mittened hands. I got in and sat as close to my door as I could. Two pro football players could have fit between us.

"You don't really need those mittens," I told her. "Your hands will sweat. You've got on too much clothes. Did Molly tell you to wear all that?"

She nodded.

"You've got to be careful about Molly. You can't believe everything she says. Wait'll you see what she's got on. She won't be all bundled up, I bet. I bet she'll have on her little blue skirt and those kind of skin-colored tights."

She pulled the mittens off and stuffed them in her pockets but didn't say anything. She looked at me funny.

Actually, she looked at me funny a couple of times, like she was trying to figure out if my head was on upside down or something. That's when I decided that Molly had been talking to her about me, too.

"OK," I said, "what did she tell you? Did she explain that I was dumb and stupid or did she just say that my first name is really Hobart?"

She smiled. Then she laughed. "Molly says you're really weird."

I crossed one eye and pretended to take my thumb apart, the old take-your-thumb-apart trick. "Weird? I don't know where she got that."

Amber giggled.

"Did she say weird was awful?"

"Not exactly."

"When you're weird you're not like everybody

else." If Molly was going to explain things to her, I would, too. She was probably a Dumb and Stupid like me. "You don't want to be like everybody else, do you?"

She thought about it. "Yes. Sometimes."

"That's because you're a girl, and girls are always doing things exactly like other girls."

"That's a dumb thing to say."

"Well, you've been doing exactly what Molly said to do all week long."

She crossed her arms tight and glared at me. "I have not."

"You have, too. And she keeps you from talking to the other girls. I noticed. She pulls you around like a dog on a leash."

"That's not true. Molly's been nice to me, but I do exactly what I want to do!"

"Amber!" Mrs. Murnyak called through the window in front of me. "Amber, dear, why don't you show Herbie that funny mint trick you did your science project on. I knew you'd want to show the children, so I put a whole package of mints in your pocket. And why don't you take off one of those heavy sweaters before you melt away? I swear," she said to my mother, "that child can be so stubborn. Sometimes she doesn't have the sense she was born with. . . ."

"OK, Mom, OK, I'm taking it off." She said it, but she didn't do it.

"It's HO-bie," I told Mrs. Murnyak, and she looked behind her to see who I was talking about. "My name's Hobie, not Herbie."

"Tie this on your bottom," one of Amber's little sisters said, and they tried to push a cushion in the car window.

"So it won't freeze to the ice," the other one shouted. Amber raised the window to seal the pillow out. I thought the twins would both die laughing.

"Mom," I told her, loud, "all of Lisa's pizza is going to be gone. There won't be anything left but a stack of smelly anchovies, and I'm starved."

She took the hint, told Mrs. Murnyak she'd call her with a plumber's number, waved everyone good-bye, scooted back in front of the wheel, and drove off. For a block she hummed as we rode. Then she turned on the radio to a station that was playing golden oldies.

"I didn't mean to bug you. I'm sorry," I told Amber.

She shrugged.

"Is there really a mint trick?" I asked her. "What do you do? Do you make them spin or turn into flying saucers or what?"

"It's not a trick, really." She smiled. "My mother was just trying to keep me from shouting at you."

"Have you *got* any mints?" My stomach had stopped growling and started barking.

"Not sure," my mom called back, thinking I was talking to her. "Didn't know you were that hungry. Hold on a minute." She started singing along with the radio.

"I'll look." Amber dug around in her pocket and pulled out a whole roll of Wint O Green Life Savers.

"Well, I don't know what trick you know with those," I told her, "but I know one—how to make them disappear."

"You want one?" She peeled open the top.

I took out a little white wheel. "Now you see it!" With my mouth open like a basketball hoop, I tossed it in the air. It landed behind my shoulder and slid into the seat crack. "And now you don't." I dug it out, threw it up again, and this time caught it on my tongue, folded it back, and crunched it into splinters. My mouth tasted like I'd just brushed my teeth.

"The old almost-never-fail disappearing-mint trick! Now, what's yours?"

"Actually," she said, "it's just like yours. Only I don't call it the disappearing-mint trick. And you don't have to throw it in the air, you just chew it."

"Here's the candy, Hobie. Be sure to share," my mom called at me, like I was three years old. "Catch." She tossed half a roll of sugar-free mints into the backseat.

The car stopped at a light, and Mom turned around to smile at us kindly, as if she could tell we were talking now the way proper children with good manners should. "Are you planning to skate tonight?" she raised her voice to ask Amber over an Elvis Presley flashback.

"I'm going to try," Amber answered politely but loud. "Molly says it's easy, that all I have to do is step out on the ice and glide."

"Do you believe that?" I asked her.

She shook her head. "I'm going to fall flat," she said. "I know it. I'm going to fall on my face, or worse."

I shrugged. She probably would. "OK," I said as we started off again, "I bite. What do *you* call it when you chew up a mint?"

I offered her one of Mom's and she took it. "This kind won't work," she said. "And mine won't actually work now. Later. In the dark."

"Later? In the dark?" And this kid thought *I* was weird. She was bananas, a whole stalk of bananas. "Why do a trick in the dark?" I asked her. "Unless you're going to cheat."

"It's got to be dark," she said. "Otherwise it's nothing." And she told me what the trick was. I didn't believe her at first. But then she even told me *how* it worked. I mean, scientific stuff. It seemed too crazy to be true.

"Are you sure?" I asked her.

"Of course I'm sure."

"And the sugar-free *won't* work?"

"I told you why."

"Look, you wouldn't want to sell me the rest of your Life Savers, would you?" I asked her as we rounded the curve in front of the community center.

"I'll give them to you if you really want them."

"No, I'll pay," I told her. I dug out the fifty cents I'd brought along in case I got starved for potato chips, and I gave it to her for the rest of her mints. Then I asked her not to tell anybody else the secret until the party was over.

"It's not a secret," she said. "Anybody might know it."

"Anybody might *not,* too. Do you swear not to tell the others?"

"Why not?"

"I've got an idea or two."

"Can't I even tell Molly?"

"Especially not Molly. Listen, are you going to spend the whole year just telling things to Molly?"

"Of course not." She put her mittens back on. "You don't plan to tell them the candy's poison because it does that, are you?"

"I haven't decided." The possibilities for those mints were huge. I hadn't even thought about saying they were poison. But nothing would work if she was going around explaining it. I held the candy out to her. "Look, if you want to show everybody the trick, that's OK."

"No," she said. "The whole thing was my mom's idea. She must have thought it would be an ice-breaker. But I can do that by falling down." She sighed. "I knew moving here was going to be hard, but I never thought I'd worry about just standing up."

"OK," I tried, "what if I hold you up one time

around the rink? And then what if you don't tell about the trick?"

She thought about it. "You mean a kind of trade?"

I nodded. Maybe we could skate when nobody was looking.

"You're not going to do anything mean with the mints, are you?"

I gave her my "Who me, innocent old me?" look.

"All right, I won't tell Molly—"

"Won't tell *anyone,*" I corrected her.

"Won't tell anyone," she said, "about what happens when Hobie—not Herbie—makes mints meet teeth." She grinned.

I didn't. "This isn't some kind of zany joke, is it?" I asked her.

Mom pulled up at the curb, switched off the radio, and turned around. "Well, here we are. Good luck," she told Amber.

"Thanks, Mrs. Hanson," Amber said. "I may not need it, though. Hobie has said he'll skate with me."

My mother smiled at my wonderful new manners.

7

·····

Double Dog Dare

The second I slammed the car door I knew I'd made a dumb mistake. I mean, at first I could just see the faces of all the kids when I pulled the mint trick on them. What a laugh. But how did I know it would work? How did I know Amber wasn't just putting me on? Besides, it probably wouldn't be all that funny. No way was even a big laugh worth keeping this kid's head above her toes her first time out on ice.

Let Molly do that. She was the one who'd said skating was no big deal.

I told Mom she could pick me up at nine thirty, but that Amber would probably get a ride home with some girls. And I was about to explain to Amber that I was just kidding about the Life Saver promise when I saw the community center door swing shut behind her.

"How's *that* for manners?" I said to Mom. But I walked in slow motion up the sidewalk so nobody looking could possibly guess I'd come in the same car with a girl.

Inside, I zigzagged down the long ramp that leads to the big changing room. It's got this neat floor made of rubber pads that fit together like pieces of a jigsaw puzzle. And it's got these benches covered with tight-weave carpet, for when you're putting on your skates. The floor is rubber and the benches are covered with carpet so you won't kill your blades. Sometimes guys in skates stand on the benches. Sometimes they even run on the benches until somebody yells at them to stop.

The place is practically home to a lot of kids who've been going there for lessons or hockey games two or three times a week since they were in kindergarten. They own their own skates. Not me. I walked over and paid a dollar to the man at the rental counter for a pair of size eights.

"Is it really true we'd do anything, even come to this party, for a piece of anchovy pizza and a couple of butterscotch brownies?" Marshall was behind me, his skates slung over his shoulder. "Is this crazy or what? Is it too late to back out?"

"Is it too late to *head* out?" I asked him. "That would be quicker."

And that's what I should have done, head out, but I didn't. Instead, we followed our feet around a corner and down a long hall to the party room. A fat green ribbon hung on the door over a sign that said HAIL QUEEN LISA!

We cracked the door a couple of inches to spy in. Nobody was hailing. Twisted strands of green and white crepe paper hung low across the ceiling. A bunch of adult types were sitting at a table near the door, eating from a box of Kentucky Fried Chicken. The girls were bunched up at one end of the room and the boys at the other. All of them were chewing on thin wedges of pizza. The room was quiet.

"If we move fast," Marshall whispered, "nobody will know we were ever—"

"Marshall! Hobie! You're late!" Lisa pulled the door all the way open and beamed us in. "There are only, like, three pizzas left!" She ran over to the table to show us.

We saw two Lisas run. Both of them had on short gold skating dresses that kind of fluttered. Both of them had on gold tights. And both of them wore gold crowns with points in the front. Actually, there were also doubles of Marshall and me staring at Lisa, doubles of all the kids, of Michelle and Jenny wearing pink skating skirts and knee guards, of all the chicken eaters, of all the crepe-paper streamers, even. The reason is that one whole wall of the room was total mirror. I stuck my tongue out at it. It didn't like me much, either.

In the daytime the party room was the dance classroom. I guess the tap dancers and ballet people really needed to see if their toes were all pointed in the same direction or if their smiles matched, but the mirror did crazy things to a party. At first it made you want to push your nose flat or stare at yourself doing Up-in-the-Air-Junior-Birdman, but before long you got tired of seeing every bite you took and itch you scratched. It was instant replay.

"Are we going to sing 'Happy Queen Day to You'?" Marshall asked after he'd folded a slice of pizza in half and swallowed it, small dead fish and all.

"I think that would be lovely," Lisa's mother told him. "Do have another piece," she said. "There's plenty." So he did that instead of singing.

Molly had cornered Amber away from the other girls, probably feeding her dog biscuits or something to keep her in line. Pretty soon I'd tell them it was just a joke, my saying I'd skate with her. Molly would laugh, so Amber would laugh. Everybody would have a big ha-ha, and it would be all over.

"Brownies, everybody," Mrs. Soloman called, uncovering a sugar-sprinkled mountain of them. "Butterscotch brownies with chocolate chips." In one minute flat the mountain was bulldozed. Some kids grabbed four.

"Well," she went on, staring at the empty plate, "I guess that's that. It will be twenty minutes or so before the rink opens. Do you want to go in and get your skates on, or would you like to play a little game or two?"

"Truth or Dare," R.X. yelled. "Hobie, what do you choose?" He was just kidding. You don't play Truth or Dare with parents around.

"Double Dog Dare," I said, keeping the joke in the air. Everybody laughed.

"Hobie calls Double Dog Dare," R.X. announced. "Give me a minute. That's not easy." Double Dog Dare is one of the worst things you can choose when you're really playing Truth or Dare. I mean, you can ask for Truth, Repeat, Promise, Dare, or Double Dare, and you've got to do what people say and it'll embarrass you probably. But if you call Double Dog Dare, Triple Dog Dare, or Sextuple Dog Dare, they can make you do practically *anything*. Of course, we weren't really playing.

"I don't know that game," Mrs. Soloman said. "Do you think the space is too small for Red Rover?"

"How about Tag?" I suggested.

Nick, who was polishing off his third brownie, groaned. "Cut it out," he said.

"Oh, no, not Tag," Mrs. Soloman told me. "Someone might slip and crack the mirror."

At one end of the room a guy jumped up and let a string of crepe paper fly free. A couple of girls pulled from the other end and all the streamers fell.

Somebody near the door flicked the lights off and everybody screamed. The room was in the basement, so it was almost totally dark.

"Isn't this fun!" Lisa called out from the middle of the room, but it wasn't much. Not even for her, I bet. It's hard to have fun at a party.

"Enough, enough. This wasn't the kind of game I meant at all," Lisa's mother said when the lights came on. "This is rowdy, and I don't like rowdy." She sighed like she was afraid she was in for a bad night. "Everybody get skates on, then. If you don't have a pass or if you need money to rent a pair, let me know."

"Thank you, Mrs. Soloman," I said on the way out. It didn't hurt all that much, and I figured I could tell my mom I'd been polite and she'd feel like she was doing a good job with me.

"Those were very good brownies, Mrs. Soloman," the kid behind me said—that, and "I need a ticket and some money for skates, Mrs. Soloman."

R.X. and Nick stopped me as I headed down the long hall. "Hey, Hobe," R.X. said, "nobody's asked for a Double Dog Dare for a long time. That's pretty brave. Nick and I are up for it, though. We've got the perfect one for you."

"I was just kidding. We weren't playing a real game." I poked him with my elbow. "You know we weren't."

He opened his eyes wide like he was really surprised. "What do you mean? I asked and you answered. We've got a whole room full of witnesses," he said. "You were loud and clear. We even saw you on the big screen. Right, Marshall?"

"Right," Marshall answered, but he was just passing by and didn't even know what the question was.

"OK," I said, "you guys are very funny. No kidding, but I've already gotten myself into one big mess tonight. I can't handle any more. You're not going to believe this. I don't know how it happened." What I figured was that skating with Amber would get me out of the dare. They'd think that was a riot. "See, somehow I got talked into saying I'd help the new kid stand up once around the rink." I started to laugh. These guys would help me out. I knew they would. "You wouldn't want to do it *for* me, would you? Or skate along behind? Maybe we could all three hold her up. What do you think?"

R.X. smiled. "That's good. That," he said, "is very good, almost as good as our Double Dog Dare. Not quite, but almost."

"Never been on ice before, has she?" Nick laughed out loud.

"You have a problem," R.X. said, "and we certainly don't want to make you break a promise. So, since you're in a jam, we'll do it this way. First, you take the new kid out and defy the laws of slick and gravity. Then, if you live through that, you do the Double Dog Dare and kiss Molly."

"Kiss Molly! No way!"

"No hurry," Nick said. "No hurry at all. Just so it's before we go home tonight." And they both grinned.

"The anchovies made me sick," I told them. "I may have to go home now."

8

· · ● · ·

I Scream,
You Scream,
We All Scream

"Ice cream!" Marshall yelled. "Anybody want the rest of my ice-cream bar so I can get out there and plow snow?" The guards throw you out if you take food on the ice. Actually, they throw you out if you snowplow, too—turning sharp and spraying kids with slush—but only if they catch you.

Marshall had bought the ice-cream bar so he wouldn't die of starvation. The last half of it had sat next to him on the fuzzy bench while he laced up his skates, though, so it probably needed a shave. Since nobody reached out, he took a last bite and tossed the rest into the trash as he headed toward the rink.

I was still taking off my first shoe.

"Hobie said he'd do *what*?" Molly shrieked from the next bench over. "I don't believe it." She marched toward me in her stocking feet. She'd heard about the Double Dog Dare, and she was about to yell at me. I decided to stare her down and say it wasn't true. Like I'd said she would be, she was wearing tights, her short blue skirt, and a huge Harvard sweatshirt. She looked mad.

Amber was padding along behind her in fat gray sweat socks.

"Hobie Hanson, this is some kind of joke, isn't it?" Molly demanded.

I smiled, like I didn't know what she was talking about but would be glad to laugh at a joke. I couldn't figure out how she'd found out so soon. Why would Nick and R.X. tell her?

"That was mean of you," she said. "Why did you tell poor Amber you'd teach her how to skate?"

Teach Amber? Molly didn't know about the dare

thing at all. Getting out of skating with the new kid was going to be a piece of cake. "I didn't exactly," I said.

"I told poor Amber it was some kind of joke." She put her hand on Amber's shoulder. "He was just kidding," she explained. "I've known Hobie a lot longer than you have, since second grade, and I can tell you exactly what he will and what he won't do. He doesn't skate with girls."

Amber stepped back from Molly and looked me in the eye.

"Well, I wasn't *exactly* kidding," I said. Molly thought she was so smart. Maybe she could boss Amber around but she couldn't boss me. Who was she to say what I would do and what I wouldn't and with who?

She sighed, like I was a serious dumbhead. "Well, you *do* know the difference between kidding and not kidding, don't you?"

"I know a lot," I told her. "A whole lot." That's when I decided I'd show her exactly what I knew. "I know, for instance, that no matter what those dumb IQ tests said, I'm probably smarter than you and Nick. Put together."

She smiled. "Right. I really believe you. That's

why you're not in TAG. It starts next week, you know. You aren't in it, are you?"

"Maybe," I said. "Maybe not. But I do have in my pocket a brand-new test for smart. It's just been discovered, and it proves how bright I am."

Amber grinned. "How do you know it works?" she asked.

"It better work," I told her. "It wouldn't dare not work."

"Well, what *is* it?" Molly was annoyed. "Hobie Hanson, you're making this up, aren't you? You're just jealous that you're not in the smart-kid program."

"Me, jealous? I don't *need* those classes. Medical science has proved this test. They've done experiments," I explained. "I don't know if they used rats or what, but I saw part of a TV show about it just a couple of weeks ago. It's this never-fail test, and they call it—"

I took a breath and tried to remember what Amber had called it. She was standing right behind Molly. "Look, Amber, we'll skate really soon," I told her. Molly frowned. "They call it—" Amber started to pronounce the word slowly, without making a sound, so I could read her lips.

"Tri-bo-lu-mi-nes-cence," I said. "It's called triboluminescence."

Molly narrowed her eyes. "You made that word up."

"I did not. It's a scientific word."

Amber nodded, just a little, but I could tell I'd got it right.

"Yoo-hoo, everyone on the ice now, my dears," Mrs. Soloman called into the changing room. Molly, Amber, and I were the only ones left from the party. "Lisa's about to do her dance routine."

"As soon as we get our skates on," I told her.

"Maybe we better go watch," Amber said.

"I'd do anything to get out of that," Molly said. "I've seen her do it at least twenty times. Maybe I could take the smart test, instead."

"Actually," I told her, and I started lacing up my skates, "I think Amber's right. We should watch Lisa. I bet her crown really sparkles when she spins around. You think they'll have the spotlight on?"

"She's starting!" Michelle came running in to tell us. "They're clearing the rink for her. Even the high-school kids have to get off. Come on, you guys!"

"Tell her just to go ahead without us," Molly said. "We'll catch her act the next time around." Then she turned back to me. "You're afraid for me to take that test, aren't you, Hobie? Do I have to spell that word or what? Did the rats spell it out by tapping their little feet?"

"It isn't a spelling test. It's a scientific test. Look, why don't you help Amber get her skates laced up tight so I can get her on the ice when Lisa's finished."

Molly rolled her eyes. "I don't believe you're going to do that."

I bent over my skates like I didn't care what she thought. "Fifth grade is different from fourth," I told her.

"Is the test math?" she asked. Molly shines at math.

"Forget it," I told her. "I can hear Lisa's music playing. It sounds like 'Ballerina Girl.' "

"OK, OK, where's a copy of this test?"

"In my pocket. I told you. But you can't take it here."

"Where, then?"

"I don't know. In the party room, I guess. That's the only place I can think of that's dark enough."

"Dark? I don't like the sound of this. Why does it have to be dark?"

"It just has to be," I told her, "and there has to be
a mirror. So we either go into the party room or the
boys' bathroom, and I don't think that's a very swift
idea."

"Hobie Hanson, is this some Truth or Dare?"

"No, it is not. Cross my heart. And hope to die.
Stick a needle in my eye." It wasn't either. I wasn't
going to kiss her.

She looked to see if my fingers were crossed.
"Amber has to come, too."

Amber had helped me out. I decided I could trust
her. "Why not? Who knows, she may be really
bright. *You* might even be."

"What do you think, Amber?" Molly asked her.

"Only if we hurry," Amber said. "I don't want to
miss Lisa. Couldn't we do it later?"

"There'll be too many kids around later," I said.
"We'll run."

I slipped my skates off, and we all three raced in
our socks down the long hall to the party room. It
was empty but still unlocked. Molly pulled open the
door, but we stopped before stepping in. You don't
run fast into the dark. Inside, a dim red exit sign was
the only light.

"OK," I said, blinking my eyes till I could see a little. "First, we go to the mirror."

"Shouldn't we at least turn the lights on so you can get the test out?" Molly asked.

"No need," I said. I took a deep breath. Even if nothing worked, the dark would be worth it. I felt scared the way I do before going on a roller coaster, or before hearing ghost stories in the night.

I reached into my right jacket pocket. That's where the Wint O Green Life Savers were. Prying one from the package with my thumb, I pulled it out and held it up. "In my hand," I explained, "I have a special piece of candy that tests intelligence."

"I can smell it," Molly said, "but I can't see it."

"I'll give you one in a minute," I told her. "Hold on. First, I have to tell you how it works. You bite into it. You crunch down on it really hard with your back teeth, and if it makes sparks, you're smart. Medical science says so."

Molly laughed.

So did Amber. "Amazing," she said. "I wonder who thought that up. Can you tell us why medical science says that happens?"

"Of course I can." It wasn't fair that she'd asked

that. And it wasn't fair that she'd laughed. I'd have to think of something.

"What did it say on the TV show?" Molly asked. "If there really *was* a TV show."

"Oh, there was, all right," I lied. "It was in that same series as the one you saw on television brain rot. And what it said was . . . See, what causes these sparks you're gonna see is brain *power*. They've found out that people who are really, really smart have all this energy stored up in their brains, and it's bouncing around like billions and billions of Ping-Pong balls. Usually you can't see it, of course, because it's, like, inside your head." Molly was quiet. I was glad she couldn't see the look on my face. "There's only one way you can see this super brain power, and that's by biting down on special test candy like I have in my hand."

"Where did you get it?" Molly asked.

"That's a secret. Anyway, you bite down on the test candy, and if there are so many sparks in your head that some of them escape through your teeth, *that* means your brain is dynamite. It means your IQ is . . . over 200. OK?"

Molly gasped. "Over 200!" She'd told us hers was 145. I wondered if I'd made the number too high. "Is it dangerous?" she asked finally. In the dark it sounded dangerous.

"It's candy. Look, I'm going to do it first. OK?" I asked again.

"I'm thinking," she said.

"Hurry," Amber told me. "I want to get back. Bite."

"You sure you're ready for this, Molly?" I asked her.

"Bite," she said.

My eyes were getting used to the red dark, so I could see our outlines clearly in the mirror. Staring hard at my face, I stuck the mint between my teeth and smashed it with my molars like Amber had said to, holding my mouth open so I could see.

CRUNCH!

Molly screamed. She *screamed*. It was wonderful. The scream was wonderful. The glow was Double Dog wonderful.

"I'm smart!" I yelled. "Look at that, I'm really smart!" I popped another one in and ground it between my teeth. The sparkle was blue, not like lightning exactly, not even like a lightning bug, but it was real, all right. It *could* have been genuine bright-blue smarts leaking out of my brain into my mouth.

Maybe it was true. Maybe I hadn't been making it up. "My IQ," I announced, "is *over* 200!"

"You sparked," Molly whispered.

"Yeah, wasn't that something?"

"It was triboluminescence," Amber said.

"Right," I agreed, as if that was something she'd learned from me.

"Look," Amber went on, "I feel terrible about not seeing all of Lisa's dance. I mean, this is her party, after all."

"Don't worry about Lisa," Molly told her.

"But I do. I'm going back out." She started for the door.

"You stay here with me," Molly told her, like that was that.

"I'm going back," Amber said. "This is silly. When you bite on the mint, it will do exactly the same thing for you that it did for Hobie. It's just a mint making sparks. Come on."

Molly didn't move. "If you want to be my friend, you'll stay," she told her.

"I just hope I didn't miss it all." Amber opened the door, let a slice of light in, and slipped out. The door closed tight.

"All right for you!" Molly called after her. I

thought sure she'd leave. But she didn't. "I want to make it spark, too," she said. And there we were in the dark. Molly and me. "Look, Hobie Hanson, I can tell you one thing," she said finally. "I'm smart enough not to chew on something without knowing what it is, even when it's going to tell me how amazingly smart I am. I want the lights on."

"I don't know," I said. Actually, I wanted to see the light myself. I felt a little scared. I don't know why. "Well, OK," I told her. "I guess a little light won't hurt the test. You know where it turns on?"

Amber had told Molly that the mints would spark when she bit, too. But that wasn't true. What Amber didn't know was that I wasn't going to give Molly the same candy I had chewed.

As Molly edged her way over to the switch, I pulled Mom's sugar-free mints out of my pocket. If Amber was right . . .

When the light flicked on, I tossed the package of sugar-frees to Molly.

She caught it, looked at it close, sniffed it, and then said, "You can buy this stuff at the grocery store. It is not special test candy."

"OK," I agreed. "It's regular candy, but it tests your IQ anyway. Scientists discover amazing things about ordinary stuff every day, you know that. Won't hurt to try. You and I can each bite into one at the same time and we'll see what happens."

Molly took a sugar-free mint from the package and threw me the rest. Then she turned the light off. I took a regular mint out of the other package and waited for her to come back to the mirror. "Remember, you've got to crunch hard," I warned her.

When we both stood there facing our reflections in the dark, I said, "Ready. Get set. Bite!"

We crushed those circles of candy flat. Demolition Derby. And when we did, my mouth sparkled like my head was a living, breathing supercomputer. I was star city. The mirror in front of Molly, though, stayed dumb dark, with only a little red reflected in it from the exit light.

She caught her breath. "I did it wrong," she said. "Give me another one."

I handed her another. The pizza smell in the air was gone. The room was minty now. She crunched again, by herself this time. Nothing. Not even a shine.

"It's not fair," she said. "I am, too, smart. Everybody says so. Something's wrong. Hobie Hanson, you're making it do that. You tell me right now what's wrong."

"Wrong? Nothing's wrong. It's just that I'm really smart and you're not," I explained.

"It's a trick."

"No, it's not. You saw it with your own eyes."

"Yes, but—"

She stopped. I heard the whispering, too. It was just outside the door. Then I felt the breeze as the door swung open. *It's Amber,* I thought. *It's got to be Amber.* Then I heard laughing like somebody trying to cover it up, and it didn't sound like Amber. It was really dumb being caught standing in the dark with Molly. There wasn't anyplace to hide, either. I thought about diving under the table where the pizza and brownies had been.

But the lights flashed on. Then off, then on, then off again, so my eyes couldn't catch hold of anything.

"Ohhhhhhhhhhhhhh," somebody moaned, long and low, a ghost sound. "Ohhhhhhhhhhhhhh." And then quiet. I didn't move.

I was about to make a dash for it out the open door when the lights flashed on again, this time to stay. It was R.X. who was standing at the switch. And next to him was Nick. They had silly smiles on their faces.

"Very interesting," Nick said. He and R.X. moved in front of the door, their arms crossed, barring the way.

"What happened?" R.X. asked Molly. "Anything special?"

We all three turned to look at her. She was not smiling. She stuck out her arms and pushed R.X. and Nick aside. "Don't you tell them what happened," she said to me as she walked out the door. "Hobie Hanson, don't you dare!"

9

Ready, Get Set, Glow!

"You don't have to do this," Amber said. "Honestly. Mrs. Soloman laced my skates up. She said she was sure Lisa would come over to help. I'm OK."

Her voice was shaky. She didn't sound OK. "No problem," I told her.

We were standing behind the glass looking in at the ice rink. It was filled with kids. Lisa was not coming over. She was still spinning around and around with light sparkling off her crown. Half a dozen figure skaters jumped and twirled with her in the middle of the rink inside a kind of fence of orange cones. Lisa may not have been the best one. Guys in hockey jackets played real Tag around the outside, trying not to get caught by the guards. Five girls in matching striped sweatshirts held hands to slow down the skaters who weaved back and forth behind them. Eugene slid up in front of us and pressed his nose flat against the glass.

I crossed my eyes at him.

"Let's forget it," Amber said. "I can't stand steady even on this rubber floor."

"If it won't kill me it won't kill you," I told her. After all, she *had* given me the spark secret. It was almost worth holding her up to have Molly think my IQ was 200 plus. Besides, Nick and R.X. were after me. They kept asking me questions. I hadn't actually told them I'd kissed Molly. I just asked them if they thought I'd cheat on a Double Dog Dare. And because of what Molly had said, they didn't think I had cheated. They just wanted details.

While I was lacing up my skates, Molly had come back to say she'd kill me if I told them she hadn't passed the smart test. I wasn't going to tell them about the test at all. I wasn't about to let Nick and

R.X. in on it. Then I wouldn't be able to use it again.

They were fooling around on the other side of the rink, but they'd be back soon, bugging me big time. Except for going home or hiding out in the john, propping Amber up on the ice was probably the safest thing to do.

Amber moved over to the entrance. Me, too. You could feel the cold breeze as skaters raced past. "If I closed my eyes and clicked my heels together, do you think I'd wake up in Arizona?" she asked me.

"No," I told her. "You'd end up on a yellow brick ice rink in Kansas, and there would be wicked witches."

She grinned and took a deep breath. "All right. What do I do?"

I got on the ice to wait for her. "Step right out like you had on regular shoes. No big deal," I explained. "Only, quick grab hold of the rail so you don't fall on your face."

Eugene was at the entrance, watching. "Couple of things to remember," he called. "Stand on the middle of the blade, not the edge. Keep your ankles straight. Don't lean too far back. Don't bend too far forward. Other than that, no big deal."

She nodded, straightened her back, and stepped

on the ice like maybe it would be easy after all. She was wrong. You could see the panic in her eyes even before you saw that her ankles had turned in and her knees were wobbling. She grabbed out with both hands, reached the rail, and hugged herself to it tight. "Do people do this for fun?" she asked.

"All it takes is practice," Eugene said. Then he edged over to me. "What's this about you and Molly?"

"Nothing," I whispered. "Nothing at all. A simple Double Dog Dare."

Amber tried to pull herself up on the rail and straighten her ankles. This time they bent out. She'd heard Eugene ask about Molly. "Did she laugh when you finally told her about the candy?" She was trying to pretend this was normal talk in a normal place.

"Was it about *candy*?" Eugene asked. "Nick and R.X. didn't say anything about candy."

"Look, I'm trying to teach Amber to skate. She's never been on ice before. If you want to do it, be my guest."

A kid racing by tagged Eugene. "Sorry," Eugene yelled, and hurried off at about a hundred miles an hour to tag somebody else. He raced off so fast that a guard in a bright orange jacket moved in on him, pulled him to the side, and wrote a number on his hand with a black marker. He was throwing Eugene off the ice. Guards do that. It's their job. It's like a policeman giving a traffic ticket. The number was what time he could get back on. I saw a guy once who'd been kicked off the ice so often he had numbers on his arm from his knuckles to his elbow. All from one night! Probably racing like Eugene had would only keep him off five minutes. Still, I didn't want to hang around the entrance where he could ask me questions till his penalty time was over.

"Look," I told Amber, "just grab the rail with one hand and my elbow with the other. I'll get you moving. You can't give up before you start."

She didn't grab.

"You go around once with me and after that it'll be a snap. Then Molly and the other girls will skate with you," I said.

"Molly's mad at me because I left her alone with you. Everybody else is busy. Nobody wants to skate with a kid who's got ankles like rubber bands."

"Just push and glide," I explained. "It's not all that hard." A girl about four years old zipped by so fast that, if she hadn't been four years old and cute, the guard would have thrown her off the ice, too. I

99

pointed her out to Amber. "See that little kid? If she can skate, you can skate."

She watched the girl skim around the bend. Then she got this look on her face, clenched her teeth, let go of the railing, held both her arms out for balance, leaned forward, pushed off, and fell flat.

She didn't even skid. She lay on the ice, face down, like those murdered bodies they make chalk lines around on TV. She didn't move. I got down on my knees to see if it'd knocked her out.

Michelle and Jenny skated up beside us. Lisa pushed off from the middle of the ice, one leg in the air, pointing at us like a bird dog. Kids skidded up, staring down.

Amber lifted her head a little, so I figured she was still alive. "Hobie," she said, "that was like telling me I can speak Greek because all the little kids in Greece do. I can't believe I fell for it."

"Get up," I told her. "You have to get back on a horse when it throws you."

She didn't even try to get up. "Horses don't throw me. I know how to ride horses. It's ice that throws me. Can I just scoot off?" She tried to swim her way back to the wall.

The crowd around us were watching with inter-

100

est. Some of them were laughing. She looked up, saw them, and groaned.

I thought about grabbing her leg and pulling her off the ice, but somehow that didn't seem right. I would have picked her up, but I didn't know how to start. Jenny and Michelle knew. They kneeled down, held Amber by the elbows, lifted her to her feet, linked arms with her, and started skating her around the rink. Lisa moved in front of them, skating backward and giving advice.

I followed just to see how everything was going. Except that her legs flopped like a Raggedy Ann doll's, Amber looked OK. I figured I'd done all I could and was just about to pass them by when all of a sudden these two guys came barreling flat out in front of us, riding on their bellies, arms out wide.

"It's a bird," R.X. called as he dived across the ice.

"It's a plane," Nick yelled, a foot or two behind him.

They were doing the Superman slide.

The closest guard blew his whistle. They'd get tossed off for at least half an hour. The Superman slide is big-time penalty stuff.

Lisa, still skating backward, tripped over Nick's legs and landed on top of R.X. Jenny and Michelle

101

could probably have skated around the three of them or put on their brakes, except that they had Amber and couldn't let go.

And ice is ice. They skidded into Supermen and the Queen and collapsed. The pile of kids was growing. I headed straight at them and fell, too, just to keep them company. Everybody was screaming. We were a seven-body pileup.

The guard skated up beside us. "Anybody hurt over here?" he asked. Nobody was. We were all laughing, even Lisa, whose crown hung down over one ear. "That was one dumb move," the guard went on, and we all laughed some more. "It's not funny," he said. Amber was holding her sides and hiccoughing, she was laughing so hard. All of us were flat on the ice with *her*. "Somebody could have been cut bad," the guard went on. "You guys know better than that. I'm not going to let you get away with it, either. You're off the ice for the rest of the night. You're outta here. You." He gave R.X.'s skate a sharp kick. "You." He nodded at Nick. "And you." He was pointing at me. I couldn't believe it.

"*I* didn't do anything," I told him. "Why me?"

"You look guilty," the guard said. "Off."

But even off the ice we couldn't stop laughing. Watching the girls try to keep Amber straight, we kept breaking up. She was getting better, but not much. Molly moved into the center behind the cones and spun around until her skirt stood out like a big blue mushroom.

Back in the changing room, though, the guys started bugging me again. "OK," R.X. said, "what happened with Molly?"

I kicked off my skates. "It was electric, OK? Now it's time for Nick's Truth or Dare. What do you take, Nick?"

"I don't want to play this," he said, untying his laces.

"Neither did I, but you made me. What do you take? Repeat?"

"OK, Repeat," he said. That's usually the easiest.

"Repeat," I told him. " 'I'm smarter than Hobie.' "

"But I'm not."

"You think you are."

"I don't. *You* think I think I am."

"You think you're better than I am because you're going to be in TAG."

"I don't."

"Say it."

"No."

"OK, I take back the Repeat."

"Truth, then," he said.

This, I decided, was the time for the new, almost-never-fail, sparky mint trick. "No, this time I get to choose because you backed out," I said. "It's Dare. Not even Double Dare."

"Take it," R.X. told him.

"I won't do anything else crazy on the ice," Nick said.

"Of course nothing crazy on the ice. You can't even *go* on the ice."

"Nothing with girls."

I waited a minute to scare him. "OK, nothing with girls."

"What is it?" R.X. asked. "You got one?"

"Sure I've got one. I dare you to take a test," I told Nick. "It's a brand-new test. It tells you if your IQ is over 200. Medical science just discovered it."

"Right," Nick said. "And as soon as they discovered it, they told *you.*"

"Don't act so smart," I told him.

"I'm *not!*" He was getting mad.

"Anyway, I have it and I dare you to take it. But

we've got to be in the dark. You can come, too," I told R.X.

With Nick grumbling all the way, we left our skates at the rental place and walked down the long hall to the party room. The door was closed, but the light was still on.

Just before I flipped the switch and turned the room red-dark again, I checked to make sure the sugar-free mints were in my left pocket and the Wint O Green ones in my right pocket. This time I knew just what to do.

We stood facing the mirror like I had with Molly. As I told them the brain-spark story, I flipped two mints out of the sugar-free roll and one mint out of the other.

"Soon, very soon," I told them, "we're going to know who's hot and who's not. Ready?"

"I guess," Nick said, and I gave them both their mints.

"Get set."

"I don't have to do this, do I?" R.X. asked.

"Nope."

"But I can if I want to. Actually, this is my kind of test. You don't have to think to take it. No sweat."

"Right. No sweat."

"Come *on!*" Nick was starting to get mad, and I didn't want him to just walk out.

"OK," I said. "Ready? Get set. Glow!"

We crunched those mints in one second flat. The mirror in front of two of us stayed black. The mirror in front of one of us sparkled. The blue-green light was even better than before.

"I don't believe it." Nick leaned forward and opened his mouth. "What's in these things?"

"It's what's in the brain that does it," I told him. "Smarts."

"I can fail that test as easy as I fail the others," R.X. said. "You sure that's all there is to it?"

"That's it. The Dare's over," I told him. "And now we know."

We all three blinked. Suddenly the lights turned on without us, only this time it was Molly at the door. Her Harvard sweatshirt was pulled down low over her skirt. "I thought you guys would be in here."

"This is really dumb," Nick said.

"Did you take the test?" Molly asked him.

"I dared him to and he did," I explained. "Actually, they both did." I started out the door.

"It's totally fake," Nick said.

107

"I agree," she told him.

"It's never failed yet," I called back.

Molly followed along beside me. "Did you tell them about me?"

I shook my head.

"Well, what happened when they took the test?" she asked. "Did Nick fail, too?"

"No big surprise," I told her. "I knew it would happen." I turned around to see Nick and R.X. still standing at the mirror. "When Nick bit the mint, he couldn't believe it. Even though he'd spent the whole summer at Mighty Byte, he couldn't believe it," I said. "But he sparked. He lit up like Einstein."

10
· · ● · ·
Turning Bright

"Is Frank here yet?" Miss Ivanovitch asked when class got going on Monday.

"Frank?" Marshall asked. "Nobody here by that name."

"But there must be. I got an amazing set of papers from him on the first day of school. He's a very interesting student."

"Frank who?" Lisa asked.

"Stein is his last name," Miss Ivanovitch said.

"Frank N. Stein." She smiled at me. How did she know I'd written them? Maybe she was some kind of handwriting expert. "Perhaps you'd like to hear more about this most unusual young man."

"Frank N. Stein," Nick said. "Hmmmm. Rings a bell. Big guy, is he? Kind of flat head with metal things sticking out of his neck? Arms down to his knees? Walks funny?" He shrugged. "Never seen him."

"Well, it's true nobody who looks like that is here this morning," Miss Ivanovitch said. "I wonder, though, if perhaps Hobie would read some of the things Frank wrote last Tuesday." She held the papers out to me, still smiling.

I looked them over. "I can try, but he's got monstrous handwriting," I said. "Let's see if I can make it out. Favorite subject is science. Electricity, especially, he says, tickles his brain. He's looking forward to studying the parts of the body. Also, he says that nothing much shocks him."

"Who *is* this guy?" Eugene asked.

Molly giggled. I was glad she got it.

"On the 'Tell-me-a-little-bit-about-yourself' part," I went on, "this kid Frank wrote, 'I'm thinking about transferring out of here to Transylvania. No jolt. I've got a friend there who really likes to get his teeth into things. The kids on the playground around here make fun of me. They say I haven't got my head screwed on tight. They call me Bolt Brain. But now that I've got it all together, I think what I'll do first is go to Boston and fly a kite with my cousin Benjamin Franklinstein.' "

"That kid Frank sounds just like Hobie," Nick said. Everybody laughed.

"The person who wrote that has no average head," Miss Ivanovitch said, "no matter what he thinks. I look forward to reading a lot of other things he writes this year.

"In fact, I learned a great deal about many of you from those first-day papers. I learned that Eugene speaks Korean, that he visited his grandparents in Korea last summer. I found out that Marshall wants to become a veterinarian, and that Jennifer has been taking piano lessons since she was six and practices an hour a day."

Actually, *I* didn't know most of those things. I looked around the class at the kids, wondering how much more I didn't know.

"And something especially interesting I learned about Amber," Miss Ivanovitch went on. "She didn't write about it, but from her transfer records I discovered that she won first prize in her school's science fair last year." Everybody stared at Amber, and her face turned about as red as her hair.

"What did she win with?" Marshall asked.

"Her project was about something I'd never heard of before," Miss Ivanovitch told us. "Something called triboluminescence."

Molly sucked in her breath. "Triboluminescence! You mean it's *real*?"

Miss Ivanovitch looked amazed. "You know about it, Molly?"

"A little," Molly said weakly. "I kind of hoped it was a joke."

"Oh, I don't think so," Miss Ivanovitch said. "Amber, will you tell us about it? It isn't something you made up, is it?"

Amber started fiddling with her pencil, and then she began to talk. "It's real, all right. It's kind of mysterious, though, and scientists are still trying to figure it out. They're doing lots of experiments with it. Mostly at Washington State University." She looked up. "What I studied was the triboluminescence in Wint O Green Life Savers."

Molly groaned, folded her arms, and put her head down on them.

"What happens," Amber went on, "is that when you crush sugar crystals it creates energy—positive and negative electric charges—that act like tiny lightning bolts. I mean, this sounds so hard. It isn't easy, but . . . "

"Go on," Miss Ivanovitch said. "We'll try to keep up. Maybe later you can bring some pictures to class to help us."

"OK." Amber took a deep breath. "When you bite on these mints in the dark they glow. OK? The sparkle you see comes from a combination of the flavoring and the sugar. You grind the sugar crystals with your teeth and that makes energy and the energy causes something in the flavoring to make a blue light. The something in the flavoring is called methylsalicylate."

There was this long, very long silence.

Molly had been listening with her head down on her arms. She lifted it, raised her hand, and asked slowly, "What happens if you crush a mint that doesn't have any sugar in it? One that's sugar free?"

"Nothing," Amber told her. "No sugar crystals, no sparks."

Molly narrowed her eyes at me. "You know that Frank N. Stein? I think he would be much happier in Transylvania. And safer, too."

I smiled at her and nodded. Miss Ivanovitch blinked. She didn't have a clue about what was going on.

"I'll write *triboluminescence* on the chalkboard for you," Miss Ivanovitch said. "*Triboluminescence* is a wonderful word. If you say it out loud, you'll discover how good it feels in the mouth. Some words are like that. Try it." We all rolled it around for a while. Tasted good. Like mint.

Nick held up his hand. "I didn't get all that, but there's something I want to know. Hobie said . . . some people say the mints make sparks because you're . . . because there's special stuff going on in your brain. That isn't true, is it?"

Amber cocked her head and chewed the tip of her pencil. She looked at me and said, "I hadn't really thought about it like that until last weekend, but it may be true."

114

"That's silly," Molly said. "It sparks for *every-body.*"

"Right," Amber said.

When Miss Ivanovitch turned around from writing *triboluminescence* on the board, she said, "It's the first word on your spelling list this week. Think you can handle it? I don't believe you'll find it in your dictionary. In the encyclopedia, perhaps. We'll look. I'll write the other words under it for you to copy. None of the rest of them has seventeen letters. I promise."

I broke the tip of my Ropski's Bar and Grill pencil and took it over to the sharpener, just a couple of steps from my desk. Nick stood in line in front of me. "Are you mad?" I asked him.

"You're the one who's mad," he said. "You've been treating me like I had chicken pox."

"I just don't like feeling dumb," I told him.

"You aren't dumb and you know it. I couldn't have written that stuff about Frankenstein. You're funny. A little weird, but funny."

"Kickball after school?" I asked him.

"Why not? If you don't aim the ball at the Spit Pit." The Spit Pit is this slimy staircase in back of the school you don't want to go down into to get balls out of.

"Aim at the Spit Pit? Me?" I said. "You know me better than that." And we both laughed.

"Boys!" Miss Ivanovitch moved over to the pencil sharpener, and we headed back to our seats.

Molly must have finished writing the words fast because before long she was at the pencil sharpener talking to Miss Ivanovitch. "When does TAG start?" Molly asked. "I just wanted to know."

I didn't have all the words copied, but I listened anyway. "You'll have your first meeting tomorrow after lunch. I'm sure I told you last week, Molly. In any case, while it's going to be hard keeping up with both TAG and your regular classwork, I think you'll do fine."

"Ummm," Molly said. "I also wanted to know, is Amber the third person from this room in it?"

Amber looked up. "No, I'm not," she told her.

"No," Miss Ivanovitch said. "It's you and Nick and . . ." I wondered for a second if it would be me and there had been some mistake about letting my parents know. Maybe. "And Marshall," she said.

I leaned back in my chair. *Marshall. It figures. Well,*

anyway, I thought, *Nick said I wasn't dumb, and if he's so smart, then he must know.*

"Not Amber? Are you sure?" Molly demanded. "I mean, she really knows a lot. At her old school she was in this program called EEP. It was for gifted and talented."

"No, I wasn't," Amber told her. "I just said they had that program. I didn't say I was in it. I *was* in a special program there, though. And I will be here, too. It's called LD. It's for kids with learning disabilities."

"You're kidding!" Molly shrieked, and lots of kids stopped writing to find out why.

I leaned forward. "How come?" I asked.

"Hobie," Miss Ivanovitch said, "have you finished with the spelling list?"

I think she was telling me to mind my own business.

"I have a hard time reading," Amber told me anyway. "A really hard time."

"But you knew all those words," Molly said. "You know a lot. How did you do that?"

Amber looked at me. "Mostly, I talked to people who knew about it, and my mom and dad read to me

117

about it. They let me do some experiments at the university with students who wanted to help. See, I know about triboluminescence, but I can't read the word. Most of the spelling list I can't read. Not yet."

Molly stood there and stared.

I looked away from Amber and up at the board. I could read the long word, but I didn't know what it meant. Not really. I guess we had different sparks in our heads.

11
·····●·····
All Tied Up

"Recess!" Miss Ivanovitch called. "Time to change gears."

I was sitting in the back of the room in the big blue beanbag chair, reading about how bats sleep upside down in caves, two hundred of them to a square foot. I couldn't decide if that was cozy or crowded. "Is it OK if I just stay here?" I asked her. "I don't feel like moving."

"It certainly is not OK," she said. "You all sit too

much, much too much. Out you go, double time."

We didn't double-time, and when we finally got out, a lot of kids collapsed on the grass.

"Up, up," she said. "Today we're going to do some serious running. I've noticed that a lot of you are not in peak shape. You are huffers and puffers. Too much television, I expect."

"Television rots the brain," Molly said. "Medical science has proved it."

"May not quite rot the brain," Miss Ivanovitch went on, "but it certainly doesn't build muscles in more than your thumbs. If you're not careful, you'll turn into couch potatoes."

"Miss Ivanovitch," Nick said, bouncing a tennis ball he'd brought out with him, "I think we're probably too young to be couch potatoes." He thought about it for a second. "Maybe couch potato chips." He threw the ball to her.

She caught it, threw it back fast, and he missed it. "OK, we're going to get all of you chips off the old potatoes into terrific shape this year. Lots of running and reading, less leaning into the old TV."

She divided us into relay teams. Me, Eugene, and Lisa were on the same one. Lisa's no couch potato.

120

She works out all the time. Eugene isn't the fastest kid in the world. Actually, I'm not bad.

Eugene's new fluorescent shoelaces were untied, flapping free like snakes who'd grown up in caves and carried their light with them.

We were up against two teams that were pretty swift, but when Lisa, Eugene, and I got together before taking our places, I told them, "OK, we're going to win this race easy. No problem. Run as fast as you can, but we've got it all tied up. Trust me. I know for sure."

"How do you know? Your horoscope or like that?" Lisa asked.

"Better than star stuff. Absolutely positive."

"Hobie," Eugene said, "you are *always* saying things like that. I don't think you—"

"Just *run*," I told him. "The force is with you."

"OK, folks, take your posts," Miss Ivanovitch called. "I want you to make those feet move." When we'd all taken our places on the big track, she took out her airplane whistle, yelled, "Ready! Get set!" and then she blew. *WHOOOOoeeeeee!*

Marshall, the leadoff guy for one team, was off the mark first. Amber, in the next lane over, started second, stumbling over a stone. Eugene was third. But once he did get going, he made tracks.

When Lisa took the stick from Eugene, she ran like there was a crowd of reporters waiting for her. She made up a lot of lost time, but we were still running second when she held the stick out to me. "Go!" she yelled with a big gasp.

I went, running as fast as I ever had. I saw Nick's back ahead of me coming into the home stretch. Then I came even with his shoulders. Reaching my legs out far, I dashed over the finish line just one long step ahead of him, about a mile before Molly. Lisa and Eugene were there waiting, clapping and yelling, and you'd have thought we'd won the gold.

I was still heaving for breath when I heard Miss Ivanovitch call out, "Ready! Get set!" and then blow her whistle for the next group.

"We did it!" Eugene said, slamming me on the back. "We really did win. I thought I was going to die, running so fast."

Molly, Amber, and Nick had fallen on the grass away from the race. "Mashed potatoes!" I yelled at them as Lisa, Eugene, and I wandered over, trying to breathe even, as if winning for us had been nothing, nothing at all.

"Hobie knew we'd win ahead of time," Eugene told them. "You guys didn't even need to try."

Amber sat up on her elbows. "He knew *ahead of time?*" she asked.

"You're kidding," Molly said, and she stood up to prove that her knees hadn't totally given out.

"OK," Nick said, "I'll bite. What did you do, look at us and say, 'No way those wimps are going to finish first'?"

"Right," Lisa said.

"No. Better," I told them, "much better. See, I knew ahead of time we were going to win because of this test I know about. Medical science has proved . . ." And they all started to laugh.

"Hobie," Molly warned, "I've heard the castles get very cold in Transylvania."

"Would I kid you," I asked, "again? No joke, medical science shows this test works even if you're running a relay race."

"Don't tell me," Nick said, and he held his head like he was thinking hard. "Let me guess." He looked at my feet. Nothing special there. Then he moved over to Eugene. "Ah, ha!" he shouted, reached out, and began to tie Eugene's shiny laces together. Eugene would have run, but I was holding his ankles.

"You've got it," I told Nick. "You are practically Sherlock Holmes. You have discovered that Eugene was our secret weapon. You know what Eugene's done? He's passed a test that has a pretty long name. Think you can handle it, Molly?"

She laughed. "Not if it's got more than seventeen letters."

"OK, here it is, the absolute complete truth. Eugene," I told them, "has aced the big-toe-luminescence test."

Everybody groaned but Amber. She folded her arms and wrinkled her forehead. "You're absolutely right. I've heard of it. Scientists all over the world are working on it right now. But you might kill it if you tie it in knots." She leaned over, pulled on Eugene's laces, and set the shining snakes free.

"Let's see if I've got this right." Nick grinned as we all looked down at Eugene's feet. "Big-toe-luminescence. That means you can tell you've got fast feet when . . ."

"When your big toes are so quick," Molly went on, "that all the energy in them rushes around like . . ."

125

"Like a million, zillion Ping-Pong balls bouncing," Nick shouted, "so crazy wild that it makes your shoelaces . . ."

And we all said it together. "That it makes your shoelaces glow in the dark."

Jamie Gilson

says she tries to make her readers "laugh and understand at the same time." She is the author of nine entertaining and popular novels for children, including the three previous Hobie Hanson stories—*Thirteen Ways to Sink a Sub, 4B Goes Wild,* and *Hobie Hanson, You're Weird.*

Ms. Gilson was born in Beardstown, Illinois, and grew up in small mid-western towns where her father was a flour miller. Following graduation from Northwestern University, she taught junior high school students, then wrote for Chicago radio stations WBEZ and WFMT. She has contributed articles to *Chicago* and *Metropolitan Home* magazines and currently conducts writing workshops for sixth graders.

Ms. Gilson and her husband, Jerry, have three children. They live in a suburb of Chicago.